UNGUARDED HOURS

The Strawberry Tree

Flesh and Grass

Unguarded Hours

The Strawberry Tree and *Flesh and Grass* are the first novellas to be published within what is a wider exploration of suspense in prose fiction.

Under the inspiration and guidance, and using the fine judgement of the Consultant Editor Ruth Rendell, we have invited writers to explore, within the demanding form of the short novel or novella, the ways in which suspense can be employed as a central guiding element in their fiction.

| Unguarded Hours |

Ruth Rendell
The Strawberry Tree

Helen Simpson
Flesh and Grass

Pandora
An Imprint of HarperCollins*Publishers*

Pandora Press
An Imprint of GraftonBooks
A Division of HarperCollins*Publishers*
77-85 Fulham Palace Road
Hammersmith, London W6 8JB

Published by Pandora Press 1990
3 5 7 9 10 8 6 4 2

© 1990, Kingsmarkham Enterprises Ltd and Helen Simpson

Ruth Rendell and Helen Simpson assert the moral right to
be identified as the authors of this work

A CIP catalogue record for this book
is available from the British Library

ISBN 0 04 440739 4

Printed in Great Britain by
Cambridge University Press

All rights reserved. No part of this publication may be
reproduced, stored in a retrieval system, or transmitted,
in any form or by any means, electronic, mechanical,
photocopying, recording or otherwise, without the prior
permission of the publishers.

The Strawberry Tree

RUTH RENDELL

1

THE HOTEL WHERE WE ARE STAYING WAS BUILT BY MY FATHER. EVERYONE ASSURES ME IT IS THE BEST IN LLOSAR AND IT IS CERTAINLY THE BIGGEST AND ugliest. From a distance it looks as if made of white cartridge paper or from hundreds of envelopes with their flaps open. Inside it is luxurious in the accepted way with sheets of bronze-coloured mirrors and tiles of copper-coloured marble and in the foyer, in stone vessels of vaguely Roman appearance, stands an army of hibiscus with trumpet flowers the red of soldiers' coats.

There is a pool and a room full of machines for exercise, three restaurants and two bars. A machine polishes your shoes and another makes ice. In the old days we used to watch the young men drink *palo* out of long thin bow-shaped vessels from which the liquor spouted in a curving stream. Now the hotel barman makes cocktails called *Mañanas* that are said to be famous. We tried them yesterday, sitting on the terrace at the back of the hotel. From there, if you are not gazing at the swimming pool as most people do, you can rest your eyes, in both senses, on the garden. There the arbutus has been planted and flourishes, its white flowers blooming and strawberry fruits ripening at the same time, something I have heard about but never seen before, for it is October and I was last here all those years ago in summer.

We have rooms with envelope balconies and a view of the bay. There are no fishing boats any more, the pier of the old hotel with its vine canopy is gone and the old hotel itself has become a casino. But the harbour is still there with the statue of

THE STRAWBERRY TREE

the Virgin, *Nuestra Doña de los Marineros*, where, swimming in the deep green water, Piers and Rosario and I first saw Will sitting on the sturdy stone wall.

All along the 'front', as I suppose I must call it, are hotels and restaurants, souvenir shops and tourist agencies, cafés and drinking places, where once stood a string of cottages. The church with its brown campanile and shallow pantiled roof that used to dominate this shore has been almost lost among the new buildings, dwarfed by the gigantic Thomson Holiday hotel. I asked the chambermaid if they had had jellyfish at Llosar lately but she only shook her head and muttered about *contaminación*.

The house we were lent by José-Carlos and Micaela is still there but much 'improved' and extended, painted sugar-pink and surrounded by a fence of the most elaborate wrought ironwork I have ever seen, iron lace for a giant's tablecloth around a giant's child's iced cake. I would be surprised if Rosario recognised it. Inland, things are much the same, as far as I can tell. Up to now I have not ventured there, even though we have a most efficient rented car. I climb up a little way out of the village and stare at the yellow hills, at the olive trees and junipers, and the straight wide roads which now make seams across them, but I cannot see the little haunted house, the *Casita de Golondro*. It was never possible to see it from here. A fold in the hills, crowned with woods of pine and carob, hides it. The manager of our hotel told me this morning it is now a *parador*, the first on Majorca.

When I have performed the task I came here to do I shall go and have a look at it. These state-run hotels, of which there are many on the mainland, are said to be very comfortable. We might have dinner there one evening. I shall propose it to the others. But as for removing from here to there, if any of them suggest it, I shall make up my mind to turn it down. For one thing, if I were staying there I should sooner or later have to rediscover *that* room or deliberately avoid it. The truth is I no longer want an explanation. I want to be quiet, I want, if this does not sound too ludicrous, to be happy.

My appointment in Muralla is for ten o'clock tomorrow morning with an officer of the *Guardia Civil* whose rank, I think, would

THE STRAWBERRY TREE

correspond to our detective superintendent. He will conduct me to see what is to be seen and I shall look at the things and try to remember and give him my answer. I haven't yet made up my mind whether to let the others come with me, nor am I sure they would want to come. Probably it will be best if I do this, as I have done so much in the past, alone.

2

NEARLY FORTY YEARS HAVE PASSED SINCE FIRST WE WENT TO MAJORCA, PIERS AND I AND OUR PARENTS, TO THE HOUSE OUR SPANISH COUSIN LENT us because my mother had been ill. Her illness was depression and a general feeling of lowness and lethargy, but the cause of it was a lost child, a miscarriage. Even then, before there was real need, my parents were trying to have more children, had been trying to have more, although I was unaware of this, since soon after my own birth thirteen years before. It was as if they knew, by some sad superstitious prevision, that they would not always have their pigeon pair.

I remember the letter to my father from José-Carlos. They had fought side by side in the Spanish Civil War and been fast friends and sporadic correspondents ever since, although he was my mother's cousin, not my father's. My mother's aunt had married a Spaniard from Santander and José-Carlos was their son. Thus we all knew where Santander was but had scarcely heard of Majorca. At any rate, we had to search for it on the map. With the exception of Piers, that is. Piers would have known, Piers could have told us it was the largest of the Balearic Islands, Baleares Province in the western Mediterranean, and probably too that it covered something over fourteen hundred square miles. But one of the many many nice things about my clever brother, child of good fortune, was his modesty. Handing out pieces of gratuitous information was never his way. He too stood and looked over our father's shoulder at Goodall and Darby's University Atlas, a pre-war edition giving pride of place to the British Empire and in which the Mediterranean was an unimportant inland sea. He looked, as we did, in silence.

The tiny Balearics floated green and gold on pale blue, held in the arms of Barcelona and Valencia. Majorca (Mallorca in brackets) was a planet with attendant moons: Formentera, Cabrera, but Minorca too and Ibiza. How strange it now seems that we had never heard of Ibiza, had no idea of how to pronounce it, while Minorca was just the place a chicken was named after.

José-Carlos's house was at a place called Llosar. He described it and its setting, deprecatingly, making little of the beauty, stressing rustic awkwardnesses. It was on the north-west coast, overlooking the sea, within a stone's throw of the village, but there was not much to the village, only a few little shops and the hotel. His English was so good it put us to shame, my father said. They would have to brush up their Spanish, my mother and he.

The house was ours for the months of July and August, or for us children's school holidays. We would find it very quiet, there was nothing to do but swim and lie in the sun, eat fish and drink in the local tavern, if my parents had a mind to that. In the south-east of the island were limestone caves and subterranean lakes, worth a visit if we would entrust ourselves to the kind of car we would find for hire. Tourists had begun to come, but there could not be many of these as there was only one hotel.

Llosar was marked on our map, on a northern cape of the island. The capital, Palma, looked quite big until you saw its letters were in the same size print as Alicante on the mainland. We had never been abroad, Piers and I. We were the children of war, born before it, confined by it to our own beleaguered island. And since the end of war we had been fated to wait patiently for something like this that would not cost much or demand a long-term plan.

I longed for this holiday. I had never been ill but now I dreaded some unspecified illness swooping down on me as the school term drew to its close. It was possible. Everyone, sooner or later, in those days before general immunisation, had measles. I had never had it. Piers had been in hospital for an operation the previous year but I had never so much as had my tonsils out. Anything could happen. I felt vulnerable, I lived in daily terror of the inexplicable gut pain, the rash appearing, the cough. I even began taking my temperature first thing in the morning, as my poor mother took hers, although for a different reason. They would go without me. Why not? It would be unfair to keep four people at home for the sake of one. I would be sent, after I came out of hospital, to stay with my Aunt Sheila.

What happened was rather different. We were not to be a member of the party fewer but to be joined by one more. José-Carlos's second letter was even more apologetic and this time, in my view at least, with justice. He had a request. We must of course say no at once if what he asked was unacceptable. Rosario would very much like to be at the house while we were there. Rosario loved the place so much and always stayed there in the summer holidays.

'Who is he?' I said.

'He's a girl,' my mother said. 'José-Carlos's daughter. I should think she must be fifteen or sixteen by now.'

'It's one of those Spanish names,' said my father, 'short for Maria of the something-or-other, Maria del Pilar, Maria del Consuelo, in this case Maria of the rosary.'

I was very taken aback. I didn't want her. The idea of a Spanish girl joining us filled me with dismay. I could imagine her, big and dark, with black flowing hair and tiers of skirts that would swing as she danced, a comb and mantilla, although I stopped at the rose between her teeth.

'We can write to José-Carlos and say it's not acceptable.' This seemed perfectly reasonable to me. 'He says we are to, so we can. We can do it at once and she'll know in plenty of time not to be there.'

My mother laughed. My father did not. Now, so long afterwards, I can look back and believe he already understood the way I was and it worried him. He said gently but not smiling, 'He doesn't mean it. He's being polite. It would be impossible for us to say no.'

'Besides,' said Piers, 'she may be very nice.' That was something I could never consider as possible. I was wary of almost everyone then and I have changed very little. I still prepare myself to dislike people and be disliked by them. Their uncharitableness I anticipate, their meanness and envy. When someone invites me to dinner and tells me that such-and-such an acquaintance

THE STRAWBERRY TREE

of theirs will be there, a man or a woman I shall love to meet, I invariably refuse. I dread such encounters. The new person, in my advance estimation, will be cold, self-absorbed, malicious, determined to slight or hurt me, will be handsome or beautiful, well-dressed and brilliant, will find me unattractive or stupid, will either not want to talk to me or will want to talk with the object of causing humiliation.

I am unable to help this. I have tried. Psychotherapists have tried. It is one of the reasons why, although rich beyond most people's dreams and good-looking enough, intelligent enough and able to talk, I have led until recently a lonely life, isolated, not so much neglected as the object of remarks such as:

'Petra won't come, so there is really no point in asking her,' and 'You have to phone Petra or write to her so far in advance and make so many arrangements before you drop in for a cup of tea, it hardly seems worth it.'

It is not so much that I am shy as that, cold myself, I understand the contempt and indifference of the cold-hearted. I do not want to be its victim. I do not want to be reduced by a glance, a laugh, a wounding comment, so that I shrivel and grow small. That is what the expression means: to make someone feel small. But another phrase, when someone says he wants the earth to open and swallow him up, that I understand, that is not something I long for but something which happens to me daily. It is only in this past year that the thaw has begun, the slow delayed opening of my heart.

So the prospect of the company of Rosario spoiled for me those last days before we left for Spain. She would be nicer to look at than I was. She would be taller. Later on in life the seniority of a friend is to one's advantage but not at thirteen. Rosario was older and therefore more sophisticated, more knowledgeable, superior and aware of it. The horrible thought had also struck me that she might not speak English. She would be a grown-up speaking Spanish with my parents and leagued with them in the great adult conspiracy against those who were still children.

So happy anticipation was spoiled by dread, as all my life it has been until now.

THE STRAWBERRY TREE

If you go to Majorca today special flights speed you there direct from Heathrow and Gatwick and, for all I know, Stansted too. It may well be true that more people go to Majorca for their holidays than anywhere else. When we went we had to take the train to Paris and there change on to another which carried us through France and the night, passing the walls of Carcassonne at sunrise, crossing the frontier into Spain in the morning. A small, light and probably ill-maintained aircraft took us from Barcelona to Palma and one of the hired cars, the untrustworthy rackety kind mentioned by José-Carlos, from Palma to the north.

I slept in the car, my head on my mother's shoulder, so I absorbed nothing of that countryside that was to grow so familiar to us, that was to ravish us with its beauty and in the end betray us. The sea was the first thing I saw when I woke up, of a deep, silken, peacock blue, a mirror of the bright cloudless sky. And the heat wrapped me like a shawl when I got out and stood there on dry pale stones, striped with the thin shadows of juniper trees.

I had never seen anywhere so beautiful. The shore which enclosed the bay was thickly wooded, a dark massy green, but the sand was silver. There was a skein of houses trailed along the shore, white cottages with flat pantiled roofs, the church with its clean square campanile and the hotel whose terrace, hung with vines and standing in the sea, was a combination of pier and tree house. Behind all this and beyond it, behind *us* the way we had come, a countryside of yellow hills scattered with grey trees and grey stones, stretched itself out and rolled up into the mountains. And everywhere stood the cypresses like no trees I had ever seen before, blacker than holly, thin as stems, clustered like groups of pillars or isolated like single obelisks, with shadows which by evening would pattern the turf with an endlessly repeated tracery of lines. Upon all this the sun shed a dry, white, relentless heat.

Children look at things. They have nothing else to do. Later on, it is not just a matter of this life being full of care and therefore worthless if we have no time to stand and stare. We have no time, we cannot change back, that is the way it is. When we are young, before the time of study, before love, before work and a place of our own to live in, everything is done for us. If we have happy childhoods, that is, and good parents. Our meals will be made and our beds, our clothes washed and new ones bought, the means to buy earned for us, transport provided and a roof over our heads. We need not think of these things or fret about them. Time does not press its hot breath on us, saying to us, go, go, hurry, you have things to do, you will be late, come, come, hurry.

So we can stand and stare. Or lean on a wall, chin in hands, elbows on the warm rough stone, and look at what lies down there, the blue silk sea unfolding in a splash of lace on the sand, the rocks like uncut agate set in a strip of silver. We can lie in a field, without thought, only with dreams, gazing through a thousand stems of grasses at the tiny life which moves among them as between the tree trunks of a wood. In a few years' time, a very few, it will be possible no more, as all the cares of life intrude, distract the mind and spoil the day, introducing those enemies of contemplation, boredom and cold and stiffness and anxiety.

At thirteen I was at the crossing point between then and now. I could still stand and stare, dawdle and dream, time being still my toy and not yet my master, but adult worries had begun. People were real, were already the only real threat. If I wanted to stay there, leaning on my wall, from which hung like an unrolled bolt of purple velvet the climber I learned to call the bougainvillea, it was as much from dread of meeting José-Carlos and his wife Micaela and Rosario, their daughter, as from any longing for the prolongation of my beautiful view. In my mind, as I gazed at it, I was rehearsing their remarks, designed to diminish me.

'Petra!'

My father was calling me, standing outside a white house with a balcony running all the way around it at first floor level. Cypresses banded its walls and filled the garden behind it, like spikes of dark stalagmites. There was a girl with him, smaller than me, I could tell even from that distance, small and thin and with a tiny face that looked out between great dark doors of hair, as through the opening in a gateway. Instead of guessing she was

THE STRAWBERRY TREE

Rosario, I thought she must be the child of a caretaker or cleaner. Introductions would not be made. I scarcely glanced at her. I was already bracing myself for the coming meeting, hardening myself, emptying my mind. Up through the white sunlight to the house I went and was on the step, had pushed open the front door, when he said her name to me.

'Come and meet your cousin.'

I had to turn and look then. She was not at all what I expected. People never are and I know that – I think I even knew it then – but this was a knowledge which made no difference. I have never been able to say, wait and see, make no advance judgements, reserve your defence. I managed to lift my eyes to hers. We did not shake hands but looked at each other and said hallo. She had difficulty with the H, making it too breathy. I noticed, close up beside her, that I was an inch taller. Her skin was pale with a glow behind it, her body as thin as an elf's. About the hair only I had been right and that not entirely. Rosario's hair was the colour of polished wood, of old furniture, as smooth and shining, and about ten times as long as mine. Later she showed me how she could sit on it, wrap herself in it. My mother told her, but kindly, meaning it as a compliment, that she could be Lady Godiva in a pageant. And then, of course, Piers, who knew the story properly, had to explain who Lady Godiva was.

Then, when we first met, we did not say much. I was too surprised. I must say also that I was gratified, for I had expected a young lady, an amalgam of Carmen and a nun, and found instead a child with Alice in Wonderland hair and ankle socks. She wore a little short dress and on a chain around her neck a seed-pearl locket with a picture of her mother. She preceded me into the house, smiling over her shoulder in a way unmistakably intended to make me feel at home. I began to thaw and to tremble a little, as I always do. Her parents were inside with my mother and Piers, but not to stay long. Once we had been shown where to find things and where to seek help if help were needed, they were to be off to Barcelona.

We had been travelling for a day and a night and half a day. My mother went upstairs to rest in the big bed under a mosquito net. My father took a shower in the bathroom which had no bath and where the water was not quite cold but of a delectable cool freshness. Piers said,

'Can we go in the sea?'

'If you like to.' Rosario spoke the very correct, oddly-accented English of one who has been taught the language with care but seldom heard it spoken by an English person. 'There is no tide here. You can swim whenever you want. Shall we go now and I can show you?'

'In a place like this,' said my brother, 'I should like to go in the sea every day and all day. I'd never get tired of it.'

'Perhaps not.' She had her head on one side. 'We shall see.'

We did grow tired of it eventually. Or, rather, the sea was not always the sweet buoyant blessing it appeared to be that first afternoon. A plague of jellyfish came and on another day someone thought he saw a basking shark. Fishermen complained that swimmers frightened off their catch. And, as a day-long occupation we grew tired of it. But that first time and for many subsequent times when we floated in its warm blue embrace and looked through depths of jade and green at the abounding marine life, at fishes and shells and the gleaming tendrils of subaqueous plants, all was perfect, all exceeded our dreams.

Our bodies and legs were white as fishes. Only our arms had a pale tan from the English summer. Piers had not been swimming since his illness but his trunks came up just high enough to hide the scar. Rosario's southern skin was that olive colour that changes only a little with the seasons but her limbs looked brown compared to ours. We sat on the rocks in the sun and she told us we must not leave the beach without covering ourselves or walk in the village in shorts or attempt to go in the church – this one was for me – with head and arms uncovered.

'I don't suppose I shall want to go in the church,' I said.

She looked at me curiously. She wasn't at all shy of us and what we said made her laugh. 'Oh, you will want to go everywhere. You will want to see everything.'

'Is there much to see?' Piers was already into the way of referring back to the textual evidence. 'Your father said there would only be swimming and a visit to the caves.'

'The caves, yes. We must take you to the caves. There are lots and lots of things to do here, Piers.'

It was the first time she had spoken his name. She pronounced it like the surname 'Pearce'. I saw him look at her with more friendliness, with more warmth, than before. And it is true that we are *warmed* by being called by our names. We all know people who hardly ever do it, who only do it when they absolutely must. They manage to steer conversations along, ask questions, respond, without ever using a first name. And they chill others with their apparent detachment, those others who can never understand that it is diffidence which keeps them from committing themselves to the use of names. They might get the names wrong, or use them too often, be claiming an intimacy to which they have no right, be forward, pushy, presumptuous. I know all about it for I am one of them.

Rosario called me Petra soon after that and Piers called her Rosario. I remained, of course, on the other side of that bridge which I was not to cross for several days. We went up to the house and Rosario said,

'I'm so happy you have come.'

It was not said as a matter of politeness but rapturously. I could not imagine myself uttering those words even to people I had known all my life. How could I be so forward, lay myself open to their ridicule and their sneers, *expose* myself to their scorn? Yet when they were spoken to me I felt no scorn and no desire to ridicule. Her words pleased me, they made me feel needed and liked. But that was far from understanding how to do myself what Rosario did, and forty years later I am only just learning.

'I'm so happy you have come.'

She said it again, this time in the hearing of my parents. Piers said,

'We're happy to be here, Rosario.'

It struck me then, as I saw him smile at her, that until then he had not really known any girls but me.

3

M Y BROTHER HAD ALL THE GIFTS, LOOKS, INTELLECT, CHARM, SIMPLE NICENESS AND, ADDED TO THESE, THE GENEROSITY OF SPIRIT THAT SHOULD come from being favoured by the gods but often does not. My mother and father doted on him. They were like parents in a fairy story, poor peasants who know themselves unworthy to bring up the changeling prince some witch has put into their own child's cradle.

Not that he was unlike them, having taken for himself the best of their looks, the best features of each of them, and the best of their talents, my father's mathematical bent, my mother's love of literature, the gentleness and humour of both. But these gifts were enhanced in him, he bettered them. The genes of outward appearance that met in him made for greater beauty than my mother and father had.

He was tall, taller at sixteen than my father. His hair was a very dark brown, almost black, that silky fine dark hair that goes grey sooner than any other. My father, who was not yet forty, was already grey. Piers's eyes were blue, as are all the eyes in our family except my Aunt Sheila's which are turquoise with a dark rim around the pupils. His face was not a film star's nor that of a model posing in smart clothes in an advertisement, but a Pre-Raphaelite's meticulous portrait. Have you seen Holman Hunt's strange painting of Valentine rescuing Sylvia, and the armed man's thoughtful, sensitive, gentle looks?

At school he had always been top of his class. Examinations he was allowed to take in advance of his contemporaries he always passed and passed well. He was destined to go up to Oxford at seventeen instead of eighteen. It was hard to say whether he was better at the sciences than the arts, and if it was philosophy he was to read at university, it might equally have been classical languages or physics.

Modern languages were the only subjects at which he failed to excel, at which he did no better and often less well than his contemporaries, and he was quick to point this out. That first evening at Llosar, for instance, he complimented Rosario on her English.

'How do you come to speak English so well, Rosario, when you've never been out of Spain?'

'I learn at school and I have a private teacher too.'

'We learn languages at school and some of us have private teachers, but it doesn't seem to work for us.'

'Perhaps they are not good teachers.'

'That's our excuse, but I wonder if it's true.'

He hastened to say what a dunce he was at French, what a waste of time his two years of Spanish. Why, he would barely know how to ask her the time or the way to the village shops. She looked at him in that way she had, her head a little on one side, and said she would teach him Spanish if he liked, she would be a good teacher. No English girl ever looked at a boy like that, in a way that was frank and shrewd, yet curiously maternal, always practical, assessing the future. Her brown river of hair flowed down over her shoulders, rippled down her back, and one long tress of it lay across her throat like a trailing frond of willow.

I have spoken of my brother in the past – 'Piers was' and 'Piers did' – as if those qualities he once had he no longer has, or as if he were dead. It is not my intention to give a false impression, but how otherwise can I recount these events? Things may be less obscure if I talk of loss rather than death, irremediable loss in spite of what has happened since, and of Piers's character only as it was at sixteen, making clear that I am aware of how vastly the personality changes in forty years, how speech patterns alter, specific learning is lost and huge accumulations of knowledge gained. Of Piers I felt no jealousy but I think this was a question of sex. If I may be allowed to evolve such an impossible thesis I would say that jealousy might have existed if he had been my sister. It is always possible for the sibling, the less favoured, to say to herself, ah, this is the way members of the opposite sex are treated, it is different for them, it is not that I am inferior or less loved, only different. Did I say that? Perhaps, in a deeply internal way. Certain it is that the next step was never taken; I never asked, where then are the privileges that should be accorded to my difference? Where are the special favours that come the way of daughters which their brothers miss? I accepted and I was not jealous.

At first I felt no resentment that it was Piers Rosario chose for her friend and companion, not me. I observed it and told myself it was a question of age. She was nearer in age to Piers than to me. And a question too perhaps, although I had no words for it then, of precocious sex. Piers had never had a girlfriend and she, I am sure, had never had a boyfriend. I was too young to place them in a Romeo and Juliet situation but I could see that they liked each other in the way boys and girls do when they begin to be aware of gender and the future. It did not matter because I was not excluded, I was always with them, and they were both too kind to isolate me. Besides, after a few days we found someone to make a fourth.

At this time we were still, Piers and I, enchanted by the beach and all that the beach offered: miles of shore whose surface was a combination of earth and sand and from which the brown rocks sprang like living plants, a strand encroached upon by pine trees with flat umbrella-like tops and purplish trunks. The sea was almost tideless but clean still, so that where it lapped the sand there was no scum or detritus of flotsam but a thin bubbly foam that dissolved at a touch into clear blue water. And under the water lay the undisturbed marine life, the bladder weed, the green sea grass and the weed-like trees of pleated brown silk, between whose branches swam small black and silver fish, sea anemones with pulsating whiskered mouths, creatures sheathed in pink shells moving slowly across the frondy seabed.

THE STRAWBERRY TREE

We walked in the water, picking up treasures too numerous to carry home. With Rosario we rounded the cape to discover the other hitherto invisible side, and in places where the sand ceased, we swam. The yellow turf and the myrtle bushes and the thyme and rosemary ran right down to the sand, but where the land met the sea it erupted into dramatic rocks, the colour of a snail's shell and fantastically shaped. We scaled them and penetrated the caves that pocked the cliffs, finding nothing inside but dry dust and a salty smell and, in the largest, the skull of a goat.

After three days spent like this, unwilling as yet to explore further, we made our way in the opposite direction, towards the harbour and the village where the little fishing fleet was beached. The harbour was enclosed with walls of limestone built in a horseshoe shape, and at the end of the right arm stood the statue of the Virgin, looking out to sea, her own arms held out, as if to embrace the world.

The harbour's arms rose some eight feet out of the sea, and on the left one, opposite *Nuestra Doña*, sat a boy, his legs dangling over the wall. We were swimming, obliged to swim for the water was very deep here, the clear but marbled dark green of malachite. Above us the sky was a hot shimmering silvery-blue and the sun seemed to have a palpable touch. We swam in a wide slow circle and the boy watched us.

You could see he was not Mallorquin. He had a pale freckled face and red hair. Today, I think, I would say Will has the look of a Scotsman, the bony, earnest, clever face, the pale blue staring eyes, although in fact he was born in Bedford of London-born parents. I know him still. That is a great understatement. I should have said that he is still my friend, although the truth is I have never entirely liked him, I have always suspected him of things I find hard to put into words. Of some kind of trickery perhaps, of having deep-laid plans, of using me. Ten years ago when he caused me one of the greatest surprises of my life by asking me to marry him, I knew as soon as I had recovered it was not love that had made him ask.

In those days, in Majorca, Will was just a boy on the watch for companions of his own age. An only child, he was on holiday with his parents and he was lonely. It was Piers who spoke to him.

This was typical of Piers, always friendly, warm-hearted, with no shyness in him. We girls, if we had been alone, would probably have made no approaches, would have reacted to the watchful gaze of this boy on the wall by cavorting in the water, turning somersaults, perfecting our butterfly stroke and other hydrobatics. We would have *performed* for him, like young female animals under the male eye, and when the display was over have swum away.

Contingency has been called the central principle of all history. One thing leads to another. Or one thing does not lead to another because something else happens to prevent it. Perhaps, in the light of what was to come, it would have been better for all if Piers had not spoken. We would never have come to the *Casita de Golondro*, so the things which happened there would not have happened, and when we left the island to go home we would all have left. If Piers had been less than he was, a little colder, a little more reserved, more like me. If we had all been careful not to look in the boy's direction but had swum within the harbour enclosure with eyes averted, talking perhaps more loudly to each other and laughing more freely in the way people do when they want to make it plain they need no one else, another will not be welcome. Certain it is that the lives of all of us were utterly changed, then and now, because Piers, swimming close up to the wall, holding up his arm in a salute, called out,

'Hallo. You're English, aren't you? Are you staying at the hotel?'

The boy nodded but said nothing. He took off his shirt and his canvas shoes. He stood up and removed his long trousers, folded up his clothes and laid them in a pile on the wall with his shoes on top of them. His body was thin and white as a peeled twig. He wore black swimming trunks. We were all swimming around watching him. We knew he was coming in but I think we expected him to hold his nose and jump in with the maximum of splashing. Instead, he executed a perfect dive, his body passing into the water as cleanly as a knife plunged into a pool.

Of course it was done to impress us, it was 'showing off'. But we didn't mind. We *were* impressed and we congratulated him. Rosario, treading water, clapped her hands. Will had broken the ice as skilfully as his dive had split the surface of the water.

He would swim back with us, he liked 'that end' of the beach.
'What about your clothes?' said Piers.

'My mother will find them and take them in.' He spoke indifferently, in the tone of the spoiled only child whose parents wait on him like servants. 'She makes me wear a shirt and long trousers all the time,' he said, 'because I burn. I turn red like a lobster. I haven't got as many skins as other people.

I was taken aback until Piers told me later that everyone has the same number of layers of skin. It is a question not of density but of pigment. Later on, when we were less devoted to the beach and began investigating the hinterland, Will often wore a hat, a big wide-brimmed affair of woven grass. He enjoyed wrapping up, the look it gave him of an old-fashioned adult. He was tall for his age which was the same as mine, very thin and bony and long-necked.

We swam back to our beach and sat on the rocks, in the shade of a pine tree for Will's sake. He was careful, fussy even, to see that no dappling of light reached him. This, he told us, was his second visit to Llosar. His parents and he had come the previous year and he remembered seeing Rosario before. It seemed to me that when he said this he gave her a strange look, sidelong, rather intimate, mysterious, as if he knew things about her we did not. All is discovered, it implied, and retribution may or may not come. There was no foundation for this, none at all. Rosario had done nothing to feel guilt about, had no secret to be unearthed. I noticed later he did it to a lot of people and it disconcerted them. Now, after so long, I see it as a blackmailer's look, although Will as far as I know has never demanded money with menaces from anyone.

'What else do you do?' he said. 'Apart from swimming?'

Nothing, we said, not yet anyway. Rosario looked defensive. After all, she almost lived here and Will's assumed sophistication was an affront to her. Had she not only three days before told us of the hundred things there were to do?

'They have bullfights sometimes,' Will said. 'They're in Palma on Sunday evenings. My parents went last year but I didn't. I faint at the sight of blood. Then there are the Dragon Caves.'

'*Las Cuevas del Drach*,' said Rosario.

'That's what I said, the Dragon Caves. And there are lots of other caves in the west.' Will hesitated. Brooding on what possibly was forbidden or frowned on, he looked up and said in the way that even then I thought of as sly, 'We could go to the haunted house.'

'The haunted house?' said Piers, sounding amused. 'Where's that?'

Rosario said without smiling, 'He means the *Casita de Golondro*.'

'I don't know what it's called. It's on the road to Pollença – well, in the country near that road. The village people say it's haunted.'

Rosario was getting cross. She was always blunt, plain-spoken. It was not her way to hide even for a moment what she felt. 'How do you know what they say? Do you speak Spanish? No, I thought not. You mean it is the man who has the hotel that told you. He will say anything. He told my mother he has seen a whale up close near Cabo del Pinar.'

'Is it supposed to be haunted, Rosario?' said my brother.

She shrugged. 'Ghosts,' she said, 'are not true. They don't happen. Catholics don't believe in ghosts, they're not supposed to. Father Xaviere would be very angry with me if he knew I talked about ghosts.' It was unusual for Rosario to mention her religion. I saw the look of surprise on Piers's face. 'Do you know it's one-thirty?' she said to Will, who had of course left his watch behind with his clothes. 'You will be late for your lunch and so will we.' Rosario and my brother had already begun to enjoy their particular rapport. They communicated even at this early stage of their relationship by a glance, a movement of the hand. Some sign he made, perhaps involuntary and certainly unnoticed by me, seemed to check her. She lifted her shoulders again, said, 'Later on, we shall go to the village, to the lace shop. Do you like to come too?' She added, with a spark of irony, her head tilted to one side, 'The sun will be going down, not to burn your poor skin that is so thin.'

The lace-makers were producing an elaborate counterpane for Rosario's mother. It had occurred to her that we might like to spend half an hour watching these women at work. We walked down there at about five, calling for Will at the hotel on the way.

THE STRAWBERRY TREE

He was sitting by himself on the terrace, under its roof of woven vine branches. Four women, one of whom we later learned was his mother, sat at the only other occupied table, playing bridge. Will was wearing a clean shirt, clean long trousers and his grass hat, and as he came to join us he called out to his mother in a way that seemed strange to me because we had only just met, strange but oddly endearing,

'My friends are here. See you later.'

Will is not like me, crippled by fear of a snub, by fear of being thought forward or pushy, but he lives in the same dread of rejection. He longs to 'belong'. His dream is to be a member of some inner circle, honoured and loved by his fellows, privileged to share knowledge of a secret password. He once told me, in an unusual burst of confidence, that when he heard someone he knew refer to him in conversation as 'my friend', tears of happiness came into his eyes.

While we were at the lacemakers' and afterwards on the beach at sunset he said no more about the *Casita de Golondro*, but that night, sitting on the terrace at the back of the house, Rosario told us its story. The nights at Llosar were warm and the air was velvety. Mosquitos there must have been, for we all had nets over our beds, but I only remember seeing one or two. I remember the quietness, the dark blue clear sky and the brilliance of the stars. The landscape could not be seen, only an outline of dark hills with here and there a tiny light glittering. The moon, that night, was increasing towards the full, was melon-shaped and melon-coloured.

The others sat in deckchairs, almost the only kind of 'garden furniture' anyone had in those days and which, today, you never see. I was in the hammock, a length of faded canvas suspended between one of the veranda pillars and a cypress tree. My brother was looking at Rosario in a peculiarly intense way. I think I remember such a lot about that evening because that look of his so impressed me. It was as if he had never seen a girl before. Or so I think now. I doubt if I thought about it in that way when I was thirteen. It embarrassed me then, the way he stared. She was talking about the *Casita* and he was watching her, but when she looked at him, he smiled and turned his eyes away.

THE STRAWBERRY TREE

Her unwillingness to talk of ghosts on religious grounds seemed to be gone. It was hard not to make the connection and conclude it had disappeared with Will's return to the hotel. 'You could see the trees around the house from here,' she said, 'if it wasn't night,' and she pointed through the darkness to the south-west where the mountains began. '*Casita* means "little house" but it is quite big and it is very old. At the front is a big door and at the back, I don't know what you call them, arches and pillars.'

'A cloister?' said Piers.

'Yes, perhaps. Thank you. And there is a big garden with a wall around it and gates made of iron. The garden is all trees and bushes, grown over with them, and the wall is broken, so this is how I have seen the back with the word you said, the cloisters.'

'But no one lives there?'

'No one has ever lived there that I know. But someone owns it, it is someone's house, though they never come. It is all locked up. Now Will is saying what the village people say but Will *does not know* what they say. There are not ghosts, I mean there are not dead people who come back, just a bad room in the house you must not go in.'

Of course we were both excited, Piers and I, by that last phrase, made all the more enticing by being couched in English that was not quite idiomatic. But what returns to me most powerfully now are Rosario's preceding words about dead people who come back. It is a line from the past, long-forgotten, which itself 'came back' when some string in my memory was painfully plucked. I find myself repeating it silently, like a mantra, or like one of the prayers from that rosary for which she was named. Dead people who come back, lost people who are raised from the dead, the dead who return at last.

On that evening, as I have said, the words which followed that prophetic phrase affected us most. Piers at once asked about the 'bad' room but Rosario, in the finest tradition of tellers of ghost stories, did not admit to knowing precisely which room it was. People who talked about it said the visitor knows. The room would declare itself.

'They say that those who go into the room never come out again.'

We were suitably impressed. 'Do you mean they disappear, Rosario?' asked my brother.

'I don't know. I cannot tell you. People don't see them again – that is what they say.'

'But it's a big house, you said. There must be a lot of rooms. If you knew which was the haunted room you could simply avoid it, couldn't you?'

Rosario laughed. I don't think she ever believed any of it or was ever afraid. 'Perhaps you don't know until you are in this room and then it is too late. How do you like that?'

'Very much,' said Piers. 'It's wonderfully sinister. Has anyone ever disappeared?'

'The cousin of Carmela Valdez disappeared. They say he broke a window and got in because there were things to steal, he was very bad, he did no work.' She sought for a suitable phrase and brought it out slightly wrong. 'The black goat of the family.' Rosario was justly proud of her English and only looked smug when we laughed at her. Perhaps she could already hear the admiration in Piers's laughter. 'He disappeared, it is true, but only to a prison in Barcelona, I think.'

The meaning of *golondro* she refused to tell Piers. He must look it up. That way he would be more likely to remember it. Piers went to find the dictionary he and Rosario would use and there it was: a whim, a desire.

'The little house of desire,' said Piers. 'You can't imagine an English house called that, can you?'

My mother came out then with supper for us and cold drinks on a tray. No more was said about the *Casita* that night and the subject was not raised again for a while. Next day Piers began his Spanish lessons with Rosario. We always stayed indoors for a few hours after lunch, siesta time, the heat being too fierce for comfort between two and four. But adolescents can't sleep in the daytime. I would wander about, fretting for the magic hour of four to come round. I read or wrote in the diary I was keeping or gazed from my bedroom window across the yellow hills with their crowns of grey olives and their embroidery of bay and juniper, like dark upright stitches on a tapestry, and now I knew of its existence, speculated about the location of the house with the sinister room in it.

THE STRAWBERRY TREE

Piers and Rosario took over the cool white dining room with its furnishings of dark carved wood for their daily lesson. They had imposed no embargo on others entering. Humbly, they perhaps felt that what they were doing was hardly important enough for that, and my mother would go in to sit at the desk and write a letter while Concepçion, who cleaned and cooked for us, would put silver away in one of the drawers of the press or cover the table with a clean lace cloth. I wandered in and out, listening not to Rosario's words but to her patient tone and scholarly manner. Once I saw her correct Piers's pronunciation by placing a finger on his lips. She laid on his lips the finger on which she wore a ring with two tiny turquoises in a gold setting, holding it there as if to model his mouth round the soft guttural. And I saw them close together, side by side, my brother's smooth dark head, so elegantly shaped, Rosario's crown of red-brown hair, flowing over her shoulders, a cloak of it, that always seemed to me like a cape of polished wood, with the depth and grain and gleam of wood, as if she were a nymph carved from the trunk of a tree.

So they were together every afternoon, growing closer, and when the lesson was over and we emerged all three of us into the afternoon sunshine, the beach or the village or to find Will by the hotel, they spoke to each other in Spanish, a communication from which we were excluded. She must have been a good teacher and my brother an enthusiastic pupil, for he who confessed himself bad at languages learned fast. Within a week he was chattering Spanish, although how idiomatically I never knew. He and Rosario talked and laughed in their own world, a world that was all the more delightful to my brother because he had not thought he would ever be admitted to it.

I have made it sound bad for me, but it was not so bad as that. Piers was not selfish, he was never cruel. Of all those close to me only he ever understood my shyness and my fears, the door slammed in my face, the code into whose secrets, as in a bad dream, my companions have been initiated but I have not. Half an hour of Spanish conversation and he and Rosario remembered their manners, their duty to Will and me, and we were back to the language we all had in common. Only once did Will have occasion to say,

'We all speak English, don't we?'

It was clear, though, that Piers and Rosario had begun to see Will as there for me and themselves as there for each other. They passionately wanted to see things in this way, so very soon they did. All they wanted was to be alone together. I did not know this then, I would have hated to know it. I simply could not have understood, though now I do. My brother, falling in love, into first love, behaved heroically in including myself and Will, in being polite to us and kind and thoughtful. Between thirteen and sixteen a great gulf is fixed. I knew nothing of this but Piers did. He knew there was no bridge of understanding from the lower level to the upper, and accordingly he made his concessions.

On the day after the jellyfish came and the beach ceased to be inviting, we found ourselves deprived, if only temporarily, of the principal source of our enjoyment of Llosar. On the wall of a bridge over a dried-up river we sat and contemplated the arid but beautiful interior, the ribbon of road that traversed the island to Palma and the side-track which led away from it to the northern cape.

'We could go and look at the little haunted house,' said Will.

He said it mischievously to 'get at' Rosario, whom he liked no more than she liked him. But instead of reacting with anger or with prohibition, she only smiled and said something in Spanish to my brother.

Piers said, 'Why not?'

4

THEY WERE VERY BEAUTIFUL, THOSE JELLYFISH. Piers kept saying they were. I found them repulsive. Once, much later, when I saw one of the same species in a marine museum I felt sick. My throat closed up and seemed to stifle me, so that I had to leave. *Phylum cnidaria*, the medusa, the jellyfish. They are named for the Gorgon with her writhing snakes for hair, a glance at whose face turned men to stone.

Those which were washed up in their thousands on the shore at Llosar were of a glassy transparency the colour of an aquamarine, and from their umbrella-like bodies hung crystalline feelers or stems like stalactites. Or so they appeared when floating below the surface of the blue water. Cast adrift on the sand and rocks, they slumped into flat gelatinous plates, like collapsed blancmanges. My kind brother, helped by Will, tried to return them to the water, to save them from the sun, but the creeping sea, although nearly tideless, kept washing them back. It was beyond my understanding that they could bear to touch that quivering clammy jelly. Rosario too held herself aloof, watching their efforts with a puzzled amusement.

By the following day a great stench rose from the beach where the sun had cooked the medusas and was now hastening the process of rot and destruction. We kept away. We walked to the village and from there took the road to Pollença which passed through apricot orchards and groves of almond trees. The apricots were drying on trays in the sun, in the heat which was heavy and unvarying from day to day. We had been in Llosar for two weeks and all that time we had never seen a cloud in the sky. Its blueness glowed with the hot light of an invisible sun. We only saw the sun when it set and dropped into the sea with a fizzle like red-hot iron plunged into water.

The road was shaded by the fruit trees and the bridge over the bed of the dried-up river, by the dense branches of pines. Here, where we rested and sat and surveyed the yellow hillsides and the olive groves, Will suggested we go to look at 'the little haunted house' and my brother said, 'Why not?' Rosario was smiling a small secret smile and as we began to walk on, Will and I went first and she and Piers followed behind.

It was not far to the *Casita de Golondro*. If it had been more than two kilometres, say, I doubt if even 'mad tourists', as the village people called us, would have considered walking it in that heat. There was a bus which went to Palma but it had left long before we started out. Not a car passed us and no car overtook us. It is hard to believe that in Majorca today. Of course there were cars on the island. My parents had several times rented a car and a driver and two days afterwards we were all to be driven to the Dragon Caves. But motor transport was unusual, something to be stared at and commented upon. As we came to the side road which would lead to the *Casita*, an unmetalled track, a car did pass us, an aged Citroën, its black bodywork much scarred and splintered by rocks, but that was the only one we saw that day.

The little haunted house, the little house of a whim, of desire, was scarcely visible from this road. A dense concentrated growth of trees concealed it. This wood, composed of trees unknown to us, carob and holm oak and witches' pines, could be seen from Llosar, a dark opaque blot on the bleached yellows and greys, while the house could not. Even here the house could only be glimpsed between tree trunks, a segment of wall in faded ochreish plaster, a shallow roof of pantiles. The plastered wall which surrounded the land which Piers called the 'demesne' was too high for any of us to see over, and our first sight of the *Casita* was through the broken bars and loops and curlicues of a pair of padlocked wrought iron gates.

We began to follow the wall along its course which soon left the road and climbed down the hillside among rocky outcroppings and stunted olive trees, herb bushes and myrtles, and in many places split open by a juniper pushing aside in its vigorous growth stones and mortar. If we had noticed the biggest of these fissures from the road we might have saved ourselves half a kilometre's walking. Only Rosario objected as Will began to climb through. She said something about our all being too old for this sort of thing but my brother's smile – she saw it too – told us how much this amused him. It was outside my understanding then but not now. You see, it was very unlike Piers to enter into an adventure of this kind. He really would have considered himself too old and too responsible as well. He would have said a gentle 'no' and firmly refused to discuss the venture again. But he had agreed and he had said, 'Why not?' I believe it was because he saw the *Casita* as a place where he could be alone with Rosario.

Oh, not for a sexual purpose, for making love, that is not what I mean. He would not, surely, at that time, at that stage of their relationship, have thought in those terms. But only think, as things were, what few opportunities he had even to talk to her without others being there. Even their afternoon Spanish lessons were subject to constant interruption. Wherever they went I or Will and I went with them. On the veranda, in the evenings, I was with them. It would not have occurred to me not to be with them and would have caused me bitter hurt, as my brother knew, if the most tactful hint was dropped that I might leave them on their own. I think it must be faced too that my parents would not at all have liked the idea of their being left alone together, would have resisted this vigorously even perhaps to the point of taking us home to England.

Had he talked about this with Rosario? I don't know. The fact is that she was no longer opposed to taking a look at the 'little haunted house' while formerly she had been very positively against it. If Piers was in love with her she was at least as much in love with him. From a distance of forty years I am interpreting words and exchanged glances, eyes meeting and rapturous looks, for what they were, the signs of first love. To me then they meant nothing unless it was that Piers and Rosario shared some specific knowledge connected with the Spanish language which gave them a bond from which I was shut out.

THE STRAWBERRY TREE

The garden was no longer much more than a walled-off area of the hillside. It was irredeemably overgrown. Inside the wall a few trees grew of a kind not to be seen outside. Broken stonework lay about among the myrtles and arbutus, the remains of a fountain and moss-grown statuary. The air was scented with bay which did not grow very profusely elsewhere and there were rosy pink heathers in flower as tall as small trees. Paths there had once been but these were almost lost under the carpet of small tough evergreens. In places it was a battle to get through, to push a passage between thorns and bay and laurels, but our persistence brought us through the last thicket of juniper into a clearing paved in broken stone. From there the house could suddenly be seen, alarmingly close to us, its cloisters only yards away. It was like being in a dream where distance means very little and miles are crossed in an instant. The house appeared, became visible, as if it had stepped out to meet us.

It was not a 'little' house. This is a relative term and the people who named it may have owned a palace somewhere else. To me it seemed a mansion, bigger than any house I had ever been in. José-Carlos's villa in Llosar and our house in London could have both been put inside the *Casita* and lost somewhere among its rooms.

Its surface was plastered and the plaster in many places had fallen away, exposing pale brickwork beneath. The cloisters were composed of eight arches supported on pillars Will said were 'Moorish', though without, I am sure, quite knowing what this meant. Above was a row of windows, all with their shutters open, all with stone balconies, a pantiled over-hang, another strip of plaster, carved or parged in panels, and above that the nearly flat roof of pink tiles.

Within the cloister, on the left-hand side of a central door, was (presumably) the window that Carmela Valdez's cousin had broken. Someone had covered it with a piece of canvas nailed to the frame, plastic not being in plentiful supply in those days. Will was the first of us to approach nearer to the house. He was wearing his grass hat and a long-sleeved shirt and trousers. He picked at the canvas around the broken window until a corner came away, and peered in.

'There's nothing inside,' he said. 'Just an old empty room. Perhaps it's *the* room.'

'It's not.' Rosario offered no explanation as to how she knew this.

'I could go in and open the door for you.'

'If it's *the* room you won't come out again,' I said.

'There's a table in there with a candle on it.' Will had his head inside the window frame. 'Someone's been eating and they've left some bread and stuff behind. What a stink, d'you reckon it's rats?'

'I think we should go home now.' Rosario looked up into Piers's face and Piers said very quickly,

'We won't go in now, not this time. Perhaps we won't ever go in.'

Will withdrew his head and his hat fell off. 'I'm jolly well going in sometime. I'm not going home without getting in there. We go back home next week. If we go now I vote we all come back tomorrow and go in there and explore it and then we'll *know*.'

He did not specify exactly what it was we should know but we understood him. The house was a challenge to be accepted. Besides we had come too far to be daunted now. And yet it remains a mystery to me today that we, who had the beaches and the sea, the countryside, the village, the boats which would take us to Pinar or Formentor whenever we wished to go, were so attracted by that deserted house and its empty rooms. For Piers and Rosario perhaps it was a trysting place but what was there about it so inviting, so enticing, to Will and me?

Will himself expressed it, in words used by many an explorer and mountaineer. 'It's *there*.'

On the following day we all went to the *Cuevas del Drach*. Will's parents, whom our parents had got to know, came too and we went in two cars. Along the roadside between C'an Picafort and Arta grew the arbutus that Will's mother said would bear white flowers and red fruit simultaneously in a month or two. I wanted to see that, I wondered if I ever would. She said the fruit was like strawberries growing on branches.

'They look like strawberries but they have no taste.'

That is one of the few remarks of Iris Harvey's I can remember.

THE STRAWBERRY TREE

Remember word for word, that is. It seemed sad to me then but now I see it as an aphorism. The fruit of the arbutus is beautiful, red and shiny, it looks like strawberries but it has no taste.

The arbutus grew only in this part of the island, she said. She seemed to know all about it. What she did not know was that these same bushes grew in profusion around the little haunted house. I identified them from those on the road to C'an Picafort, from the smooth glossy leaves that were like the foliage of garden shrubs, not wild ones. Among the broken stones, between the junipers and myrtle, where all seemed dust-dry, I had seen their leaves, growing as green as if watered daily.

On our return we inspected the beach and found the jellyfish almost gone, all that remained of them gleaming patches on the rocks like snail's trails. Piers and Rosario sat on the veranda doing their Spanish and Will went back to the hotel, his shirt cuffs buttoned, his hat pulled well down.

'Tomorrow then,' Piers had said to him as he left and Will nodded.

That was all that was necessary. We did not discuss it among ourselves. A decision had been reached, by each of us separately and perhaps simultaneously, in the cars or the caves or by the waters of the subterranean lake. Tomorrow we should go into the little haunted house, to see what it was like, because it was *there*. But a terrible or wonderful thing happened first. It was terrible or wonderful, depending on how you looked at it, how *I* looked at it, and I was never quite sure how that was. It filled my mind, I could scarcely think of anything else.

My parents had gone to bed. I was in the bedroom I shared with Rosario, not in bed but occupied with arranging my mosquito net. This hotel where we now are is air-conditioned, you never open the windows. You move and dress and sleep in a coolness which would not be tolerated in England, a breezy chill that is very much at odds with what you can see beyond the glass, cloudless skies and a desiccated hillside. I liked things better when the shutters could be folded back against the walls, the casements opened wide, and the net in place so that you were protected from insects, yet in an airy room. The net hung rather like curtains do from a tester on an English four-poster and that morning, in a hurry to be off to the *Cuevas*, I had forgotten to close them.

Having made sure there were no mosquitos inside the curtains, I drew them and switched off the light so that no more should be attracted into the room. Sentimentally, rather than kill it, I carried a spider in my handkerchief to the window to release it into the night. The moon was waxing, a pearl drop, and the stars were brilliant. While dark, with a rich clear somehow shining darkness, everything in the little walled garden could clearly be seen. All that was missing was not clarity but colour. It was a monochrome world out there, black and silver and pewter and pearl and lead-colour and the opaque velvety greyness of stone. The moon glowed opal-white and the stars were not worlds but light-filled holes in the heavens.

I did not see them at first. I was looking past the garden at the spread of hills and the mountains beyond, serrated ranges of darkness against the pale shining sky, when a faint sound or tiny movement nearer at hand drew my eyes downwards. They had been sitting together on the stone seat in the deep shade by the wall. Piers got up and then Rosario did. He was much taller than she, he was looking down at her and she up at him, eye to eye. He put his arms round her and his mouth on hers and for a moment, before they stepped back into the secretive shadow, they seemed to me so close that they were one person, they were like two cypresses intertwined and growing as a single trunk. And the shadow they cast was the long spear shape of a single cypress on moon-whitened stone.

I was very frightened. I was shocked. My world had changed in a moment. Somewhere, I was left behind. I turned away with the shocked rejecting movement of someone who has seen a violent act. Once inside my mosquito net, I drew its folds about me and lay hidden in there in the dark. I lay there rigid, holding my hands clasped, then turned on to my face with my eyes crushed into the pillow.

Rosario came upstairs and into our room and spoke softly to me but I made her no answer. She closed the door and I knew she was undressing in the dark. In all my life I had never felt so lonely. I would never have anyone, I would always be alone. Desertion presented itself to me as a terrible reality to be confronted, not to be avoided, and the last image that was before me when sleep came was of getting up in the morning and finding them all gone, my parents and Piers and Rosario, the hotel empty, the village abandoned, Majorca a desert island and I its only wild, lost, crazed inhabitant. Not quite the last image. That was of the twin-trunked cypress tree in the garden, its branches interwoven and its shadow a single shaft.

5

WE ENTERED THE LITTLE HOUSE OF DESIRE, THE LITTLE HAUNTED HOUSE (*LA CASITA QUE TIENE FANTASMAS*) BY THE FRONT DOOR, ROSARIO GOING first. Will had climbed in through the broken window and opened the door inside the cloisters. It had the usual sort of lock which can be opened by turning a knob on the inside but from the outside only with a key. Piers followed her and I followed him, feeling myself to be last, the least there, the unwanted.

This, of course, was not true. The change was in my mind, not in outward reality. When I got up that morning it was not to find myself deserted, abandoned in an alien place by all those close to me, but treated exactly as usual. Piers was as warm to me as ever, as *brotherly*, my parents as affectionate, Rosario the same kind and interested companion. I was different. I had seen and I was changed.

As I have said, I could think of nothing else. What I had seen did not excite or intrigue me, nor did I wish not to have seen it, but rather that it had never happened. I might have been embarrassed in their company but I was not. All I felt, without reason, was that they liked each other better than they liked me, that they expressed this in a way neither of them could ever have expressed it to me, and that, obscurely but because of it, *because of something he did not and could not know*, Will too must now prefer each of them to me.

On the way to the *Casita* I had said very little. Of course I expected Piers to ask me what was the matter. I would have told him a lie. That was not the point. The point was that I was unable to understand. Why, why? What made them do that, behave in the way I had seen them in the garden? Why had they spoiled things? For me, they had become different people. They were strangers. I saw them as mysterious beings. It was my first glimpse of the degree to which human beings are unknowable, my first intimation of what it is that makes for loneliness. But what I realised at the time was that we who had been a cohesive group were now divided into two parts: Piers and Rosario, Will and me.

Yet I had not chosen Will. We *choose* very few of the people we know and call our friends. In various ways they have been thrust upon us. We never have the chance to review a hundred paraded before us and out of them choose one or two. I knew nothing of this then and I resented Will for being Will, cocky, intrusive, with his red hair and his thin vulnerable skin, his silly hat, and for being so much less nice to know than either my brother or Rosario. But he was for me and they were not, not any more. I sensed that he felt much the same way about me. I was the third best but all he could get, his companion by default. This was to be my future lot in life – and perhaps his, but I cared very little about that. It was because of this, all this, that as we entered the *Casita*, Piers and Rosario going off into one of the rooms, Will making for the hall at the front of the house, I left them and went up the staircase on my own.

I was not afraid of the house, at least not then. I was too sore for that. All my misery and fear derived from human agency, not the supernatural. If I thought of the 'bad room' at all, it was with that recklessness, that fatalism, which comes with certain kinds of unhappiness: things are so bad that *anything* which happens will be a relief – disaster, loss, death. So I climbed the stairs and explored the house, looking into all the rooms, without trepidation and without much interest.

It was three storeys high. With the exception of a few objects difficult to move or detach, heavy mirrors on the walls in gilded frames, an enormous bed with black oak headboard and bedposts, a painted wooden press, it was not furnished. I heard my brother's and Rosario's voices on the staircase below and I knew somehow that Piers would not have remained in the house and would not have let us remain if there had been furniture and carpets and pictures there. He was law-abiding and responsible. He would not have trespassed in a place he saw as someone's home.

But this house had been deserted for years. Or so it seemed to me. The mirrors were clouded and blue with dust. The sun bore down unchecked by shutters or curtains and its beams were layers of sluggishly moving dust that stretched through spaces of nearly intolerable heat. I suppose it was because I was a child from a northern country that I associated hauntings with cold. Although everything I had experienced since coming to Llosar taught otherwise, I had expected the *Casita de Golondro* to be cold inside and dark.

The heat was stifling and the air was like a gas. What you breathed was a suspension of warm dust. The windows were large and hazy dusty sunshine filled the house, it was nearly as light as outside. I went to the window in one of the rooms on the first floor, meaning to throw it open, but it was bolted and the fastenings too stiff for me to move. It was there, while I was struggling with the catch, that Will crept up behind me and when he was only a foot away made that noise children particularly associate with ghosts, a kind of warbling crescendo, a howling siren-sound.

'Oh, shut up,' I said. 'Did you think I couldn't hear you? You made more noise than a herd of elephants.'

He was undaunted. He was never daunted. 'Do you know the shortest ghost story in the world? There was this man reached out in the dark for a box of matches but before he found them they were stuck into his hand.'

I pushed past him and went up the last flight of stairs. Piers and Rosario were nowhere to be seen or heard. I saw the double cypress tree again and its shadow and felt sick. Somewhere they were perhaps doing that again now, held close together, looking into each other's eyes. I stood in the topmost hallway of the house, a voice inside me telling me what it has often told me since, when human relations are in question: don't think of them, forget them, stand alone, you are safer alone. But my brother. . ? It was different with my brother.

The rooms on the top floor had lower ceilings, were smaller than those below and even hotter. It sounds incomprehensible if

THE STRAWBERRY TREE

I say that these attics were like cellars, but so it was. They were high up in the house, high under the roof, but they induced the claustrophobia of basements, and there seemed to be weighing on them a great pressure of tiers of bricks and mortar and tiles.

What happened to me next I feel strange about writing down. This is not because I ever doubted the reality of the experience or that time has dimmed it but really because, of course, people don't believe me. Those I have told – a very few – suggest that I was afraid, expectant of horrors, and that my mind did the rest. But I was *not* afraid. I was so unafraid that even Will's creeping up on me had not made me jump. I was expectant of nothing. My mind was full of dread but it was dread of rejection, of loneliness, of others one by one discovering the secret of life and I being left in ignorance. It was fear of losing Piers.

All the doors to all the rooms had been open. In these circumstances, if you then come upon a closed door, however miserable you may be, however distracted, natural human curiosity will impel you to open it. The closed door was at the end of the passage on the left. I walked down the passage, through the stuffiness, the air so palpable you almost had to push it aside, tried the handle, opened the door. I walked into a rather small oblong room with, on its left-hand wall, one of those mirrors, only this one was not large or gilt-framed or fly-spotted, but rather like a window with a plain wooden frame and a kind of shelf at the bottom of it. I saw that it was a mirror but I did not look into it. Some inner voice was warning me not to look into it.

The room was dark. No, not dark, but darker than the other rooms. Here, although apparently nowhere else, the shutters were closed. I took a few steps into the warm gloom and the door closed behind me. Hindsight tells me that there was nothing supernatural or even odd about this. It had been closed while all the others in the house were open which indicates that it was a 'slamming' door or one which would only remain open when held by a doorstop. I did not think of this then. I thought of nothing reasonable or practical, for I was beginning to be frightened. My fear would have been less if I could have let light in but the shutters, of course, were on the outside of the window. I have said it was like a cellar up there. I felt as if I was in a vault.

THE STRAWBERRY TREE

Something held me there as securely as if I were chained. It was as if I had been tied up preparatory to being carried away. And I was aware that behind me, or rather to the left of me, was that mirror into which I must not look. Whatever happened I must not look into it and yet something impelled me to do so, I *longed* to do so.

How long did I stand there, gasping for breath, in that hot timeless silence? Probably for no more than a minute or two. I was not quite still, for I found myself very gradually rotating, like a spinning top that is slowing before it dips and falls on its side. Because of the mirror I closed my eyes. As I have said, it was silent, with the deepest silence I have ever known, but the silence was broken. From somewhere, or inside me, I heard my brother's voice. I heard Piers say,

'Where's Petra?'

When I asked him about this later he denied having called me. He was adamant that he had not called. Did I imagine his voice just as I then imagined what I saw? Very clearly I heard his voice call me, the tone casual. But concerned, for all that, caring.

'Where's Petra?'

It broke the invisible chains. My eyes opened on to the hot, dusty, empty room. I spun round with one hand out, reaching for the door. In doing so I faced the mirror, I moved through an arc in front of the mirror, and saw, not myself, *but what was inside it.*

Remember that it was dark. I was looking into a kind of swimming gloom and in it the room was reflected but in a changed state, with two windows were no windows were, and instead of myself the figure of a man in the farthest corner pressed up against the wall. I stared at him, the shape or shade of a bearded ragged man, not clearly visible but clouded by the dark mist which hung between him and me. I had seen that bearded face somewhere before – or only in a bad dream? He looked back at me, a look of great anger and malevolence. We stared at each other and as he moved away from the wall in my direction, I had a momentary terror he would somehow break through the mirror and be upon me. But, as I flinched away, holding up my hands, he opened the reflected door and disappeared.

THE STRAWBERRY TREE

I cried out then. No one had opened the door on my side of the mirror. It was still shut. I opened it, came out and stood there, my back to the door, leaning against it. The main passage was empty and so was the side passage leading away to the right. I ran along the passage, feeling I must not look back, but once round the corner at the head of the stairs I slowed and began walking. I walked down, breathing deeply, turned at the foot of the first flight and began to descend the second. There I met Piers coming up.

What I would best have liked was to throw myself into his arms. Instead, I stopped and stood above him, looking at him.

'Did you call me?' I said.

'No. When do you mean? Just now?'

'A minute ago.'

He shook his head. 'You look as if you've seen a ghost.'

'Do I?' Why didn't I tell him? Why did I keep silent? Oh, I have asked myself enough times. I have asked myself why that warning inner voice did not urge me to tell and so, perhaps, save him. No doubt I was afraid of ridicule, for even then I never trusted to kindness, not even to his. 'I went into a room,' I said, 'and the door closed on me. I was a bit scared, I suppose. Where are the others?'

'Will found the haunted room. Well, he says it's the haunted room. He pretended he couldn't get out.'

How like Will that was! There was no chance for me now, even if I could have brought myself to describe what had happened. My eyes met Piers's eyes and he smiled at me reassuringly. Never since in all my life have I so longed to take someone's hand and hold it as I longed then to take my brother's. But all that was possible for me was to grip my own left hand in my right and so hold everything inside me.

We went down and found the others and left the house. Will pinned the canvas back over the broken window and we made our way home in the heat of the day. The others noticed I was unusually quiet and they said so. There was my chance to tell them but of course I could not. Will had stolen a march on me. But there was one curious benefit deriving from what had happened to me in the room with the closed shutters and the slamming door. My jealousy, resentment, insecurity I suppose we would call it now, over Piers and Rosario had quite gone. The new anxiety had cast the other out.

Nothing would have got me back to the *Casita*. As we walked across the hillside, among the prickly juniper and the yellow broom, the green-leaved arbutus and the sage, I was cold in the hot sun, I was staring ahead of me, afraid to look back. I did not look back once. And later that day, gazing across the countryside from my bedroom window, although the *Casita* was not visible from there, I would not even look in its direction, I would not even look at the ridge of hillside which hid it.

That evening Piers and Rosario went out alone together for the first time. There was no intention to deceive, I am sure, but my parents thought they had gone with me and Will and Will's mother to see the country dancing at Muro. It was said the *ximbombes* would be played and we wanted to hear them. Piers and Rosario had also shown some interest in these Mallorquin drums but they had not come with us. Will thought they had gone with my parents to see the Roman theatre, newly excavated at Puerto de Belver, although by then it was too dark to see anything.

When we got home they were already back. They were out on the veranda, sitting at the table. The moon was bright and the cicadas very noisy and of course it was warm, the air soft and scented. I had not been alone at all since my experience of the morning and I did not want to be alone then, shrouded by my mosquito net and with the moonlight making strange patterns on the walls. But almost as soon as I arrived home Rosario got up and came upstairs to bed. We hardly spoke, we had nothing to say to each other any more.

Next evening they went out together again. My father said to Piers,

'Where are you going?'

'For a walk.'

THE STRAWBERRY TREE

I thought he would say, 'Take Petra', because that was what he was almost certain to say, but he did not. His eyes met my mother's. Did they? Can I remember that? I am sure their eyes must have met and their lips twitched in small indulgent smiles.

It was moonlight. I went upstairs and looked out of the window of my parents' room. The village was a string of lights stretched along the shore, a necklace in which, here and there, beads were missing. The moon did not penetrate these dark spaces. A thin phosphorescence lay on the calm sea. There was no one to be seen. Piers and Rosario must have gone the other way, into the country behind. I thought, suppose I turn round and there, in the corner of this room, in the shadows, that man is.

I turned quickly and of course there was nothing. I ran downstairs and to while away the evening, my parents and I, we played a lonely game of beggar-my-neighbour. Piers and Rosario walked in at nine. On the following day we were on the beach where Will, for whom every day was April Fool's Day, struck dismay into our hearts with a tale of a new invasion of jellyfish. He had seen them heading this way from the hotel pier.

This was soon disproved. Will was forgiven because it was his next but last day. He boasted a lot about what he called his experiences in the 'haunted room' of the *Casita* two days before, claiming that he had had to fight with the spirits who tried to drag him through the wall. I said nothing, I could not have talked about it. When siesta time came I lay down on my bed and I must have slept, for Rosario had been on the other bed but was gone when I awoke, although I had not heard or seen her leave.

They were gone, she and my brother, when I came downstairs and the rest of us were preparing to go with Will and his parents in a hired car to see the gardens of a Moorish estate.

'Piers and Rosario won't be coming with us,' my mother said, looking none too pleased, and feeling perhaps that politeness to the Harveys demanded more explanation, 'They've found some local fisherboy to take them out in his boat. They said, would you please excuse them.'

Whether this fisherboy story was true or not, I don't know. I suspect my mother invented it. She could scarcely say – well, not in those days – 'My son wants to be alone with his girlfriend.' Perhaps there was a boy and a boat and perhaps this boy was questioned when the time came. I expect everyone who might have seen or spoken to Piers and Rosario was questioned, everyone who might have an idea of their whereabouts, because they never came back.

6

IN THOSE DAYS THERE WERE FEW EATING PLACES ON THE ISLAND, JUST THE DINING ROOMS OF THE BIG HOTELS OR SMALL LOCAL *TABERNAS*. ON OUR WAY BACK from the Moorish gardens we found a restaurant, newly opened with the increase of tourism, at a place called Petra. Of course this occasioned many kindly jokes on my name and the proprietor of the *Restorán del Toro* was all smiles and welcome.

Piers and Rosario's evening meal was to have been prepared by Concepçion. She was gone when we returned and they were still out. My parents were cross. They were abstracted and unwilling to say much in front of me, although I did catch one sentence, an odd one and at the time incomprehensible.

'Their combined ages only add up to thirty-one!'

It is not unusual to see displeasure succeeded by anxiety. It happens all the time. *They're late, it's inexcusable, where are they, they're not coming, something's happened.* At about half-past nine this change-over began. I was questioned. Did I have any idea where they might be going? Had they said anything to me?

We had no telephone. That was far from unusual in a place like that forty years ago. But what use could we have put it to if we had had one? My father went out of the house and I followed him. He stood there looking up and down the long shoreline. We do this when we are anxious about people who have not come, whose return is delayed, even though if they are there, hastening towards us, we only shorten our anxiety by a moment or two. They were not there. No one was there. Lights were on in the houses and the strings of coloured lamps interwoven with the vine above the hotel pier, but no people were to be seen. The waning moon shone on an empty beach where the tide crawled up a little way and trickled back.

Apart from Concepçion, the only people we really knew were Will's parents and when another hour had gone by and Piers and Rosario were not back my father said he would walk down to the hotel, there to consult with the Harveys. Besides, the hotel had a phone. It no longer seemed absurd to talk of phoning the police. But my father was making a determined effort to stay cheerful. As he left, he said he was sure he would meet Piers and Rosario on his way.

No one suggested I should go to bed. My father came back, not with Will's parents who were phoning the police 'to be on the safe side', but with Concepçion at whose cottage in the village he had called. Only my mother could speak to her but even she could scarcely cope with the Mallorquin dialect. But we soon all understood, for in times of trouble language is transcended. Concepçion had not seen my brother and cousin that evening and they had not come for the meal she prepared for them. They had been missing since five.

That night remains very clearly in my memory, every hour distinguished by some event. The arrival of the police, the searching of the beach, the assemblage in the hotel foyer, the phone calls that were made from the hotel to other hotels, notably the one at Formentor, and the incredible inefficiency of the telephone system. The moon was only just past the full and shining it seemed to me for longer than usual, bathing the village and shoreline with a searching whiteness, a providential floodlighting. I must have slept at some point, we all must have, but I remember the night as white and wakeful. I remember the dawn coming with tuneless birdsong and a cool pearly light.

The worst fears of the night gave place in the warm morning to what seemed like more realistic theories. At midnight they had been dead, drowned, but by noon theirs had become a voluntary flight. Questioned, I said nothing about the cypress tree, entwined in the garden, but Will was not so reticent. His last day on the island had become the most exciting of all. He had seen Piers and Rosario kissing, he said, he had seen them holding hands.

Rolling his eyes, making a face, he said they were 'in lo-ove'. It only took a little persuasion to extract from him an account of our visit to the *Casita* and a quotation from Piers, probably Will's own invention, to the effect that he and Rosario would go there to be alone.

The *Casita* was searched. There was no sign that Piers and Rosario had been there. No fisherman of Llosar had taken them out in his boat, or no one admitted to doing so. The last person to see them, at five o'clock, was the priest who knew Rosario and who had spoken to her as they passed. For all that, there was for a time a firm belief that my brother and Rosario had run away together. Briefly, my parents ceased to be afraid and their anger returned. For a day or two they were angry, and with a son whose behaviour had scarcely ever before inspired anger. He who was perfect had done this most imperfect thing.

Ronald and Iris Harvey postponed their departure. I think Iris liked my mother constantly telling her what a rock she was and how we could not have done without her. José-Carlos and Micaela were sent for. As far as I know they uttered no word of reproach to my parents. Of course, as far as I know is not very far. And I had my own grief – no, not that yet. My wonder, my disbelief, my panic.

Piers's passport was not missing. Rosario was in her own country and needed no passport. They had only the clothes they were wearing. Piers had no money, although Rosario did. They could have gone to the mainland of Spain. Before the hunt was up they had plenty of time to get to Palma and there take a boat for Barcelona. But the police found no evidence to show that they had been on the bus that left Llosar at six in the evening, and no absolute evidence that they had not. Apart from the bus the only transport available to them was a hired car. No one had driven them to Palma or anywhere else.

The difficulty with the running away theory was that it did not at all accord with their characters. Why would Piers have run away? He was happy. He loved his school, he had been looking forward to this sixth form year, then to Oxford. My mother said, when Will's mother presented to her yet again the 'Romeo and Juliet' theory,

'But we wouldn't have stopped him seeing his cousin. We'd have invited her to stay. They could have seen each other every holiday. We're not strict with our children, Iris. If they were really that fond of each other, they could have been engaged in a few years. But they're so young!'

At the end of the week a body was washed up on the beach at Alcudia. It was male and young, had a knife wound in the chest, and for a few hours was believed to be that of Piers. Later that same day a woman from Muralla identified it as a man from Barcelona who had come at the beginning of the summer and been living rough on the beach. But that stab wound was very ominous. It alerted us all to terrible ideas.

The *Casita* was searched again and its garden. A rumour had it that part of the garden was dug up. People began remembering tragedies from the distant past, a suicide pact in some remote inland village, a murder in Palma, a fishing boat disaster, a mysterious unexplained death in a hotel room. We sat at home and waited and the time our departure from the island was due, came and went. We waited for news, we three with José-Carlos and Micaela, all of us but my mother expecting to be told of death. My mother, then and in the future, never wavered in her belief that Piers was alive and soon to get in touch with her.

After a week the Harveys went home, but not to disappear from our lives. Iris Harvey had become my mother's friend, they were to remain friends until my mother's death, and because of this I continued to know Will. He was never very congenial to me, I remember to this day the *enjoyment* he took in my brother's disappearance, his unholy glee and excitement when the police came, when he was permitted to be with the police on one of their searches. But he was in my life, fixed there, and I could not shed him. I never have been able to do so.

One day, about three weeks after Piers and Rosario were lost, my father said,

'I am going to make arrangements for us to go home on Friday.'

'Piers will expect us to be here,' said my mother. 'Piers will write to use here.'

My father took her hand. 'He knows where we live.'

'I shall never see my daughter again,' Micaela said. 'We shall never see them again, you know that, we all know it, they're dead and gone.' And she began crying for the first time, the unpractised sobs of the grown-up who has been tearless for years of happy life.

My father returned to Majorca after two weeks at home. He stayed in Palma and wrote to us every day, the telephone being so unreliable. When he wasn't with the police he was travelling about the island in a rented car with an interpreter he had found, making enquiries in all the villages. My mother expected a letter by every post, not from him but from Piers. I have since learned that it is very common for the mothers of men who have disappeared to refused to accept that they are dead. It happens all the time in war when death is almost certain but cannot be proved. My mother always insisted Piers was alive somewhere and prevented by circumstances from coming back or from writing. What circumstances these could possibly have been she never said and arguing with her was useless.

The stranger thing was that my father, who in those first days seemed to accept Piers's death, later came part of the way round to her opinion. At least, he said it would be wrong to talk of Piers as dead, it would be wrong to give up hope and the search. That was why, during the years ahead, he spent so much time, sometimes alone and sometimes with my mother, in the Balearics and on the mainland of Spain.

Most tragically, in spite of their brave belief that Piers would return or the belief that they *voiced*, they persisted in their determination to have more children, to compensate presumably for their loss. At first my mother said nothing of this to me and it came as a shock when I overheard her talking about it to Iris Harvey. When I was fifteen she had a miscarriage and later that year, another. Soon after that she began to pour out to me her hopes and fears. I cannot have known then that my parents were doomed to failure but I seemed to know, I seemed to sense in my gloomy way perhaps, that something so much wished-for would never happen. It would not be allowed by the fates who rule us.

'I shouldn't be talking like this to you,' she said, and perhaps she was right. But she went on talking like that. 'They say that

THE STRAWBERRY TREE

longing and longing for a baby prevents you having one. The more you want the less likely it is.'

This sounded reasonable to me. It accorded with what I knew of life.

'But no one tells you how to stop longing for something you long for,' she said.

When they went to Spain I remained behind. I stayed with my Aunt Sheila who told me again and again she thought it a shame my parents could not be satisfied with the child they had. I should have felt happier in her house if she had not asked quite so often why my mother and father did not take me with them.

'I don't want to go back there,' I said. 'I'll never go back.'

7

THE LOSS OF HIS SON MADE MY FATHER RICH. HIS WEALTH WAS THE DIRECT RESULT OF PIERS'S DISAPPEARANCE. IF PIERS HAD COME BACK THAT NIGHT we should have continued as we were, an ordinary middle-class family living in a semi-detached suburban house, the breadwinner a surveyor with the local authority. But Piers's disappearance made us rich and at the same time did much to spoil Spain's Mediterranean coast and the resorts of Majorca.

He became a property developer. José-Carlos, already in the building business, went into partnership with him, raised the original capital, and as the demands of tourism increased, they began to build. They built hotels: towers and skyscrapers, shoe-box shapes and horseshoe shapes, hotels like ziggurats and hotels like Piranesi palaces. They built holiday flats and plazas and shopping precincts. My father's reason for going to Spain was to find his son, his reason for staying was this new enormously successful building enterprise.

He built a house for himself and my mother on the north-west coast at Puerto de Soller. True to my resolve I never went there with them and eventually my father bought me a house in Hampstead. He and my mother passed most of their time at Puerto de Soller, still apparently trying to increase their family, even though my mother was in her mid-forties, still advertising regularly for Piers to come back to them, wherever he might be. They advertised, as they had done for years, in the *Majorca Daily Bulletin* as well as Spanish national newspapers and *The Times*. José-Carlos and Micaela, on the other hand, had from the first given Rosario up as dead. My mother told me they never spoke of her. Once, when a new acquaintance asked Micaela if she had any children, she had replied with a simple no.

If they had explanations for the disappearance of Piers and Rosario, I never heard them. Nor was I ever told what view was taken by the National Guard, severe brisk-spoken men in berets and brown uniforms. I evolved theories of my own. They *had* been taken out in a boat, had both drowned and the boatman been too afraid later to admit his part in the affair. The man whose body was found had killed them, hidden the bodies and then killed himself. My parents were right up to a point and they had run away together, being afraid of even a temporary enforced separation, but before they could get in touch had been killed in a road accident.

'That's exactly when you would know,' Will said. 'If they'd died in an accident that's when it would have come out.'

He was on a visit to us with his mother during the school summer holidays, a time when my parents were always in England. The mystery of my brother's disappearance was a subject of unending interest to him. He never understood, and perhaps that kind of understanding was foreign to his nature, that speculating about Piers brought me pain. I remember to this day the insensitive terms he used. 'Of course they've been bumped off,' was a favourite with him, and 'They'll never be found now, they'll just be bones by now.'

But equally he would advance fantastic theories of their continued existence. 'Rosario had a lot of money. They could have gone to Spain and stopped in a hotel and stolen two passports. They could have stolen passports from the other guests. I expect they earned money singing and dancing in cafés. Spanish people like that sort of thing. Or she could have been someone's maid. Or an artist's model. You can make a lot of money at that. You sit in a room with all your clothes off and people who're learning to be artists sit round and draw you.'

Tricks and practical jokes still made a great appeal to him. To stop him making a phone call to my mother and claiming to be, with the appropriate accent, a Frenchman who knew Piers's whereabouts, I had to enlist the help of his own mother. Then, for quite a long time, we saw nothing of Ronald and Iris Harvey or Will in London, although I believe they all went out to Puerto Soller for a holiday. Will's reappearance in my life was heralded by the letter of condolence he wrote to me seven years later when my mother died.

He insisted then on visiting me, on taking me about, and paying a curious kind of court to me. Of my father he said, with his amazing insensitivity,

'I don't suppose he'll last long. They were very wrapped up in each other, weren't they? He'd be all right if he married again.'

My father never married again and, fulfilling Will's prediction, lived only another five years. Will did not marry either and I always supposed him homosexual. My own marriage, to the English partner in the international corporation begun by my father and José-Carlos, took place three years after my mother's death. Roger was very nearly a millionaire by then, two-and-a-half times my age. We led the life of rich people who have too little to do with their time, who have no particular interests and hardly know what to do with their money.

It was not a happy marriage. At least I think not, I have no idea what other marriages are like. We were bored by each other and frightened of other people but we seldom expressed our feelings and spent our time travelling between our three homes and collecting seventeenth century furniture. Apart from platitudes, I remember particularly one thing Roger said to me:

'I can't be a father to you, Petra, or a brother.'

By then my father was dead. As a direct result of Piers's death I inherited everything. If he had lived or there had been others, things would have been different. Once I said to Roger,

'I'd give it all to have Piers back.'

As soon as I had spoken I was aghast at having expressed my feelings so freely, at such a profligate flood of emotion. It was so unlike me. I blushed deeply, looking fearfully at Roger for signs of dismay, but he only shrugged and turned away. It made things worse between us. From that time I began talking compulsively about how my life would have been changed if my brother had lived.

'You would have been poor,' Roger said. 'You'd never have met me. But I suppose that might have been preferable.'

That sort of remark I made often enough myself. I took no notice of it. It means nothing but that the speaker has a low self-image and no one's could be lower than mine, not even Roger's.

'If Piers had lived my parents wouldn't have rejected me. They wouldn't have made me feel that the wrong one of us died, that if I'd died they'd have been quite satisfied with the one that was left. They wouldn't have wanted more children.'

'Conjecture,' said Roger. 'You can't know.'

'With Piers behind me I'd have found out how to make friends.'

'He wouldn't have been behind you. He'd have been off. Men don't spend their lives looking after their sisters.'

When Piers and Rosario's disappearance was twenty years in the past a man was arrested in the South of France and charged with the murder, in the countryside between Bedarieux and Lodeve, of two tourists on a camping holiday. In court it was suggested that he was a serial killer and over the past two decades had possibly killed as many as ten people, some of them in Spain, one in Ibiza. An insane bias against tourists was the motive. According to the English papers, he had a violent xenophobia directed against a certain kind of foreign visitor.

This brought to mind the young man's body with the stab wound that had been washed up on the beach at Alcudia. And yet I refused to admit to myself that this might be the explanation for the disappearance of Piers and Rosario. Like my parents, Roger said, I clung to a belief, half fantasy, half hope, that somewhere they were still alive. It was a change of heart for me, this belief, it came with my father's death, as if I inherited it from him along with all his property.

And what of the haunted house, the *Casita de Golondro*? What of my strange experience there? I never forgot it, I even told Roger about it once, to have my story received with incomprehension and the remark that I must have been eating some indigestible Spanish food. But in the last year of his life we were looking for a house to buy, the doctors having told him he should not pass another winter in a cold climate. Roger hated 'abroad', so it had to be in England, Cornwall or the Channel Islands. In fact no house was ever bought, for he died that September, but in the meantime I had been viewing many possibilities and one of these was in the south of Cornwall, near Falmouth.

It was a Victorian house and big, nearly as big as the *Casita*, ugly Gothic but with wonderful views. An estate agent took me over it and, as it turned out, I was glad of his company. I had never seen such a thing before, or thought I had not, an internal room without windows. Not uncommon, the young man said, in houses of this age, and he hinted at bad design.

This room was on the first floor. It had no windows but the room adjoining it had, and in the wall which separated the two was a large window with a fanlight in it which could be opened. Thus light would be assured in the windowless room if not much air. The Victorians distrusted air, the young man explained.

I looked at this dividing window and twenty-eight years fell away. I was thirteen again and in the only darkened room of a haunted house, looking into a mirror. But now I understood. It was not a mirror. It had not been reflecting the room in which I stood but affording me a sight of a room beyond, a room with windows and another door, and of its occupant. For a moment, standing there, remembering that door being opened, not a reflected but a real door, I made the identification between the man I had seen, the man at the wheel of the battered Citroën and the serial killer of Bedarieux. But it was too much for me to take, I was unable to handle something so monstrous and so ugly. I shuddered, suddenly seeing impenetrable darkness before me, and the young man asked me if I was cold.

'It's the house,' I said. 'I wouldn't dream of buying a house like this.'

Will was staying with us at the time of Roger's death. He often was. In a curious way, when he first met Roger, before we were married, he managed to present himself in the guise of my rejected lover, the devoted admirer who knows it is all hopeless but who cannot keep away, so humble and selfless is his passion. Remarks such as 'may the best man win' and 'some men have all the luck' were sometimes uttered by him, and this from someone who had never so much as touched my hand or spoken to me a word of affection. I explained to Roger but he thought I was being modest. What other explanation could there be for Will's devotion? Why else but from long-standing love of me would he phone two or three times a week, bombard me with letters, angle for invitations? Poor Roger had made his fortune too late in life to understand that the motive for pursuing me might be money.

Roger died of a heart attack sitting at his desk in the study. And there Will found him when he went in with an obsequious cup of tea on a tray, even though we had a housekeeper to do all that. He broke the news to me with the same glitter-eyed relish as I remembered him recounting to the police tales of the little haunted house. His voice was lugubrious but his eyes full of pleasure.

Three months later he asked me to marry him. Without hesitating for a moment, I refused.

'You're going to be very lonely in the years to come.'

'I know,' I said.

8

NEVER ONCE DID I SERIOUSLY THINK OF THROWING IN MY LOT WITH WILL. BUT THAT WAS A DIFFERENT MATTER FROM TELLING HIM I HAD NO wish to see him again. He was distasteful to me with his pink face, the colour of raw veal, the ginger hair that clashed with it, and the pale blue bird's-egg eyes. His heart was as cold as mine but hard in a way mine never was. I disliked everything about him, his insensitivity, the pleasure he took in cruel words. But for all that, he was my friend, he was my only friend. He was a man to be taken about by. If he hinted to other people that we were lovers, I neither confirmed nor denied it. I was indifferent. Will pleaded poverty so often since he had been made redundant by his company that I began allowing him an income but instead of turning him into a remittance man, this only drew him closer to me.

I never confided in him, I never told him anything. Our conversation was of the most banal. When he phoned – I *never* phoned him – the usual platitudes would be exchanged and then, desperate, I would find myself falling back on that well-used silence-filler and ask him,

'What have you been doing since we last spoke?'

When I was out of London, at the house in Somerset or the 'castle', a castellated shooting lodge Roger had bought on a whim in Scotland, Will would still phone me but would reverse the charges. Sometimes I said no when the operator asked me if I would pay for the call, but Will – thick-skinned mentally, whatever his physical state might be – simply made another attempt half an hour later.

THE STRAWBERRY TREE

It was seldom that more than three days passed without our speaking. He would tell me about the shopping he had done, for he enjoys buying things, troubles with his car, the failure of the electrician to come, the cold he had had, but never of what he might understand love to be, of his dreams or his hopes, his fear of growing old and of death, not even what he had been reading or listening to or looking at. And I was glad of it, for I was not interested and I told him none of these things either. We were best friends with no more intimacy than acquaintances.

The income I allowed him was adequate, no more, and he was always complaining about the state of his finances. If I had to name one topic we could be sure of discussing whenever we met or talked it would be money. Will grumbled about the cost of living, services bills, fares, the small amount of tax he had to pay on his pension and what he got from me, the price of food and drink and the cost of the upkeep of his house. Although he did nothing for me, a fiction was maintained that he was my personal assistant, 'secretary' having been rejected by him as beneath the dignity of someone with his status and curriculum vitae. Will knew very well that he had no claim at all to payment for services rendered but for all that he talked about his 'salary', usually to complain that it was pitifully small. Having arrived – without notice – to spend two weeks with me in Somerset, he announced that it was time he had a company car.

'You've got a car,' I said.

'Yes,' he said, 'a rich man's car.'

What was that supposed to mean?

'You need to be rich to keep the old banger on the road,' he said, as usual doubling up with mirth at his own wit.

But he nagged me about that car in the days to come. What was I going to do with my money? What was I saving it for, I who had no child? If he were in my place it would give him immense pleasure to see the happiness he could bring to others without even noticing the loss himself. In the end I told him he could have my car. Instead of my giving it in part exchange for a new one, he could have it. It was a rather marvellous car, only two years old and its sole driver had been a prudent middle-aged woman, that favourite of insurers, but it was not good enough for Will. He took it but he complained and we quarrelled. I told him to get out and he left for London in my car.

Because of this I said nothing to him when the lawyer's letter came. We seldom spoke of personal things but I would have told him about the letter if we had been on our normal terms. I had no one else to tell and he, anyway, was the obvious person. But for once, for the first time in all those years, we were out of touch. He had not even phoned. The last words he had spoken to me, in hangdog fashion, sidling out of the front door, were a truculent muttered plea that in spite of everything I would not stop his allowance.

So the letter was for my eyes only, it contents for my heart only. It was from a firm of solicitors in the City and was couched in gentle terms. Nothing, of course, could have lessened the shock of it, but I was grateful for the gradual lead-up, and for such words as 'claim', 'suggest', 'allege' and 'possibility'. There was a softness, like a tender touch, in being requested to prepare myself and told that at this stage there was no need at all for me to rush into certain conclusions.

I could not rest but paced up and down, the letter in my hand. Then, after some time had passed, I began to think of hoaxes, I remembered how Will had wanted to phone my mother and give her that message of hope in a Frenchman's voice. Was this Will again? It was the solicitors I phoned, not Will, and they told me, yes, it was true that a man and a woman had presented themselves at their offices, claiming to be Mr and Mrs Piers Sunderton.

9

I AM NOT A GULLIBLE PERSON. I AM CAUTIOUS, UNFRIENDLY, MOROSE AND ANTI-SOCIAL. LONG BEFORE I BECAME RICH I WAS SUSPICIOUS. I DISTRUSTED PEOPLE and questioned their motives, for nothing had ever happened to me to make me believe in disinterested love. All my life I had never been loved but the effect of this was not to harden me but to keep me in a state of dreaming of a love I had no idea how to look for. My years alone have been dogged by a morbid fear that everyone who seems to want to know me is after my money.

There were in my London house a good many photographs of Piers. My mother had cherished them religiously, although I had hardly looked at them since her death. I spread them out and studied them, Piers as a baby in my mother's arms, Piers as a small child, a schoolboy, with me, with our parents and me. Rosario's colouring I could remember, her sallow skin and long hair, the rich brown colour of it, her smallness of stature and slightness, but not what she looked like. That is, I had forgotten her features, their shape, arrangement and juxtaposition. Of her I had no photograph.

From the first, even though I had the strongest doubts about this couple's identity as my brother and his wife, I never doubted that any wife he might have had would be Rosario. Illogical? Absurd? Of course. Those convictions we have in the land of emotion we can neither help nor escape from. But I told myself as I prepared for my taxi ride to London Wall that if it was Piers that I was about to see, the woman with him would be Rosario.

THE STRAWBERRY TREE

I was afraid. Nothing like this had happened before. Nothing had *got this far* before. Not one of the innumerable 'sightings' in those first months, in Rome, in Naples, Madrid, London, the Tyrol, Malta, had resulted in more than the occasional deprecating phone call to my father from whatever police force it might happen to be. Later on there had been claimants, poor things who presented themselves at my door and who lacked the nous even to learn the most elementary facts of Pier's childhood, fair-haired men, fat men, short men, men too young or too old. There were probably ten of them. Not one got further than the hall. But this time I was afraid, this time my intuition spoke to me, saying, 'He has come back from the dead,' and I tried to silence it, I cited reason and caution, but again the voice whispered, and this time more insistently.

They would be changed out of all knowledge. What was the use of looking at photographs? What use are photographs of a boy of sixteen in recognising a man of fifty-six? I waited in an ante-room for three minutes. I counted those minutes. No, I counted the seconds which composed them. When the girl came back and led me in, I was trembling.

The solicitor sat behind a desk and on a chair to his left and a chair to his right sat a tall thin grey man and a small plump woman, very Spanish-looking, her face brown and still smooth, her dark hair sprinkled with white pulled severely back. They looked at me and the two men got up. I had nothing to say but the tears came into my eyes. Not from love or recognition or happiness or pain but for time which does such things to golden lads and girls, which spoils their bodies and ruins their faces and lays dust on their hair.

My brother said, 'Petra,' and my sister-in-law, in that voice I now remembered so precisely, in that identical heavily-accented English, 'Please forgive us, we are so sorry.'

I wanted to kiss my brother but I could hardly go up to a strange man and kiss him. My tongue was paralysed. The lawyer began to talk for us but of what he said I have no recollection, I took in none of it. There were papers for me to see, so-called 'proofs', but although I glanced at them, the print was invisible. Speech was impossible but I could think. I was thinking, I will go to my house in the country, I will take them with me to the country.

Piers had begun explaining. I heard something about Madrid and the South of France, I heard the word 'ashamed' and the words 'too late', which someone has said are the saddest in the English language, and then I found a voice in which to say,

'I don't need to hear that now, I understand, you can tell me all that later, much later.'

The lawyer, looking embarrassed, muttered about the 'inevitable ensuing legal proceedings.'

'What legal proceedings?' I said.

'When Mr Sunderton has satisfied the court as to his identity, he will naturally have claim on your late father's property.'

I turned my back on him, for I knew Piers's identity. Proofs would not be necessary. Piers was looking down, a tired, worn-out man, a man who looked unwell. He said, 'Rosario and I will go back to our hotel now. It's best for us to leave it to Petra to say when she wants another meeting.'

'It's best,' I said, 'for us to get to know each other again. I want you both to come to the country with me.'

We went, or rather, Rosario and I went, to my house near Wincanton. Piers was rushed to hospital almost before he set foot over my threshold. He had been ill for weeks, had appendicitis which became peritonitis, and they operated on him just in time.

Rosario and I went to visit him every day. We sat by his bedside and we talked, we all had so much to say. And I was fascinated by them, by this middle-aged couple who had once like all of us been young but who nevertheless seemed to have passed from adolescence into their fifties without the intervention of youth and middle years. They had great tenderness for each other. They were perfectly suited. Rosario seemed to know exactly what Piers would want, that he only liked grapes which were seedless, that although a reader he would only read magazines in hospital, that the slippers he required to go to the day room must be of the felt not the leather kind. He disliked chocolates, it was useless bringing any.

'He used to love them,' I said.

'People change, Petra.'

'In many ways they don't change at all.'

I questioned her. Now the first shock and joy were passed I could not help assuming the role of interrogator, I could not help putting their claim to the test, even though I knew the truth so well. She came through my examination very well. Her memory of Majorca in those distant days was even better than mine. I had forgotten – although I recalled it when she reminded me – our visit to the monastery at Lluc and the sweet voices of the boy choristers. Our parents' insistence that while in Palma we all visited the *Mansion de Arte*, this I now remembered, and the Goya etchings which bored us but which my mother made us all look at.

José-Carlos and Micaela had both been dead for several years. I could tell she was unhappy speaking of them, she seemed ashamed. This brought us to the stumbling block, the difficulty which reared up every time we spoke of their disappearance. Why had they never got in touch? Why had they allowed us all, in such grief, to believe them dead?

She – and later Piers – could give me no reason except their shame. They could not face my parents and hers, it was better for us all to accept that they were dead. To explain why they had run away in the first place was much easier.

'We pictured what they would all say if we said we were in love. Imagine it! We were sixteen and fifteen, Petra. But we were right, weren't we? You could say we're still in love, so we were right.'

'They wouldn't have believed you,' I said.

'They would have separated us. Perhaps they would have let us meet in our school holidays. It would have killed us, we were dying for each other. We couldn't live out of sight of the other. That feeling has changed now, of course it has. I am not dying, am I, though Piers is in the hospital and I am here? It wasn't just me, Petra, it was Piers too. It was Piers's idea for us to – go.'

'Did he think of his education? He was so brilliant, he had everything before him. To throw it up for – well, he couldn't tell it would last, could he?'

'I must tell you something, Petra. Piers was not so brilliant as you thought. Your father had to see Piers's headmaster just before you came on that holiday. He was told Piers wasn't keeping up with his early promise, he wouldn't get that place at Oxford, the way he was doing he would be lucky to get to a university at all. They kept it a secret, you weren't told, even your mother wasn't, but Piers knew. What had he to lose by running away with me?'

'Well, comfort,' I said, 'and his home and security and me and his parents.'

'He said – forgive me – that I made up for all that.'

She was sweet to me. Nothing was too much trouble for her. I, who had spent so much time alone that my tongue was stiff from disuse, my manners reclusive, now found myself caught up in her gaiety and her charm. She was the first person I have ever known to announce in the morning *ideas* for how to spend the day, even if those notions were often only that I should stay in bed while she brought me my breakfast and then that we should walk in the garden and have a picnic lunch there. When there was a need for silence, she was silent, and when I longed to talk but scarcely knew how to begin she would talk for me, soon involving us in a conversation of deep interest and a slow realisation of the tastes we had in common. Soon we were companions and by the time Piers came home, friends.

Until we were all together again I had put off the discussion of what happened on the day they ran away. Each time Rosario had tried to tell me I silenced her and asked for more about how they had lived when first they came to the Spanish mainland. Their life at that time had been a series of adventures, some terrible, some hilarious. Rosario had a gift for story-telling and entertained me with her tales while we sat in the firelight. Sometimes it was like one of those old Spanish picaresque novels, full of event, anecdote, strange characters and hairsbreadth escapes, not all of it I am afraid strictly honest and above-board. Piers had changed very quickly or she had changed him.

They had worked in hotels, their English being useful. Rosario had even been a chambermaid. Later they had been guides, and at one time, in a career curiously resembling Will's scenario, had sung in cafés to Piers's hastily improvised guitar-playing. In her capacity as a hotel servant – they were in Madrid by this time – Rosario had stolen two passports from guests and with these they had left Spain and travelled about the South of France. The names of the passport holders became their names and in them they were married at Nice when he was eighteen and she seventeen.

'We had a little boy,' she said. 'He died of meningitis when he was three and after that no more came.'

I thought of my mother and put my arms round her. I, who have led a frozen life, have no difficulty in showing my feelings to Rosario. I, in whom emotion has been something to shrink from, can allow it to flow freely in her company and now in my brother's. When he was home again, well now and showing in his face some vestiges of the Piers I had known so long ago, I found it came quite naturally to go up to him, take his hand and kiss his cheek. In the past I had noticed, while staying in other people's houses, the charming habit some have of kissing their guests good night before everyone retires to their rooms. For some reason, a front of coldness perhaps, I had never been the recipient of such kisses myself. But now – and amazing though it was, I made the first move myself – I was kissing both of them good night and we exchanged morning kisses when we met next day.

One evening, quite late, I asked them to tell me about the day itself, the day which ended so terribly in fear and bright empty moonlight. They looked away from me and at each other, exchanging a rueful nostalgic glance. It was Rosario who began the account of it.

It was true that they had met several times since that first time in the little haunted house. They could be alone there without fear of interruption and there they had planned, always fearfully and daringly, their escape. I mentioned the man I had seen, for now I was sure it had been a man seen through glass and no ghost in a mirror, but it meant nothing to them. At the *Casita* they had always found absolute solitude. They chose that particular day because we were all away at the gardens but made no other special preparations, merely boarding the afternoon bus for Palma a little way outside the village. Rosario, as we had always known, had money. She had enough to buy tickets for them on the boat from Palma to Barcelona.

'If we had told them or left a note they would have found us and brought us back,' Rosario said simply.

She had had a gold chain around her neck with a cameo that they could sell, and a gold ring on her finger.

'The ring with the two little turquoises,' I said.

'That was the one. I had it from my grandmother when I was small.'

They had sold everything of value they had, Piers's watch and his fountain pen and his camera. The ring saved their lives, Piers said, when they were without work and starving. Later on they became quite rich, for Piers, like my father, used tourism to help him, went into partnership with a man they met in a café in Marseille, and for years they had their own hotel.

There was only one question left to ask. Why did they ever come back?

They had sold the business. They had read in the deaths column of a Spanish newspaper they sometimes saw that Micaela, the last of our parents, was dead. Apparently, the degree of shame they felt was less in respect to me. I could understand that, I was only a sister. Now I think I understood everything. Now when I looked at them both, with a regard that increased every day, I wondered how I could ever have doubted their identities, how I could have seen them as old, as unutterably changed.

The time had come to tell Will. We were on speaking terms again. I had mended the rift myself, phoning him for the first time ever. It was because I was happy and happiness made me kind. During the months Piers and Rosario had been with me he had phoned as he always did, once or twice we had met away from home, but I had not mentioned them. I did not now, I simply invited him to stay.

To me they were my brother and sister-in-law, familiar loved figures with faces already inexpressibly dear, but he I knew would not know them. I was not subjecting them to a test, I needed no test, but the idea of their confronting each other without preparation amused me. A small deception had to be practised and I made them reluctantly agree to my introducing them as 'my friends Mr and Mrs Page.'

For a few minutes he seemed to accept it. I watched him, I noticed his hands were trembling. He could bear his suspicion no longer and burst out:

THE STRAWBERRY TREE

'It's Piers and Rosario, I know it is!'

The years could not disguise them for him, although they each separately confessed to me afterwards that if they had not been told they would never have recognised him. The red-headed boy with 'one skin too few' was not just subsumed in the fat red-faced bald man but utterly lost.

Whether their thoughts often returned to those remarks the solicitor had made on the subject of legal proceedings I cannot say. When mine did for the second time I spoke out. We were too close already for litigation to be conceivable. I told Piers that I would simply divide all my property in two, half for them and half for me. They were shocked, they refused, of course they did. But eventually I persuaded them. What was harder for me to voice was my wish that the property itself should be divided in two, the London house, the Somerset farm, my New York apartment, literally split down the middle. Few people had ever wanted much of my company in the past and I was afraid they would see this as a bribe or as taking advantage of my position of power. But all Rosario said was,

'Not too strictly down the middle, Petra, I hope. It would be nicer to *share*.'

All I stipulated was that in my altered will I should leave all I possessed to my godchild and cousin, Aunt Sheila's daughter, and Piers readily agreed, for he intended to leave everything he had to the daughter of his old partner in the hotel business.

So we lived. So we have lived for rather more than a year now. I have never been so happy. Usually it is not easy to make a third with a married couple. Either they are so close that you are made to feel an intruder or else the wife will see you as an ally to side with her against her husband. And when you are young the danger is that you and the husband will grow closer than you should. With Piers and Rosario things were different. I truly believe that each wanted my company as much as they wanted each other's. In those few months they came to love me and I, who have loved no one since Piers went away, reciprocated. They have shown me that it is possible to grow warm and kind, to learn laughter and pleasure, after a lifetime of coldness. They have unlocked something in me and liberated a lively spirit that must always have been there but which languished for long years, chained in a darkened room.

It is two weeks now since the Majorcan police got in touch with me and told me what the archaeologists had found. It would be helpful to them and surely of some satisfaction to myself to go to Majorca and see what identification I could make, not of remains, it was too late for that, but of certain artefacts found in the caves.

We were in Somerset and once more Will was staying with us. I suggested we might all go. All those years I had avoided re-visiting the island but things were different now. Nothing I could see there could cause me pain. While I had Piers and Rosario I was beyond pain, it was as if I was protected inside the warm shell of their affection.

'In that case,' Will said, 'I don't see the point of going. You know the truth. These bits of jewellery, clothes, whatever they are, can't be Piers's and Rosario's because they sold theirs, so why try to identify what in fact you can't identify?'

'I want to see the place again,' I said. 'I want to see how it's changed. This police thing, that's just an excuse for going there.'

'I suppose there will be bones too,' he said, 'and maybe more than bones even after so long.' He has always had a fondness for the macabre. 'Did the police tell you how it all got into the caves?'

'Through a kind of pothole from above, they think, a fissure in the cliff top that was covered by a stone.'

'How will you feel about going back, Piers?' asked Rosario.

'I shan't know till I get there,' he said, 'but if Petra goes we go too. Isn't that the way it's always going to be?'

10

WHEN I WOKE UP THIS MORNING IT WAS WITH NO SENSE OF IMPENDING DOOM. I WAS NEITHER AFRAID NOR HOPEFUL, I WAS INDIFFERENT. THIS was no more than a chore I must perform for the satisfaction of officials, as a 'good citizen'. For all that, I found my room confining in spite of the wide-open windows, the balcony and view of the sea, and cancelling my room service order, I went down to breakfast.

To my surprise I found the others already there in the terrace dining room. It was not quite warm enough to sit outside so early. They were all unaware of my approach, were talking with heads bent and close together above the table. I was tempted to come up to them in silence and lay a light loving hand on Rosario's shoulder but somehow I knew that this would make her start. Instead I called out a 'good morning' that sounded carefree because it was.

Three worried faces were turned to me, although their frowns cleared to be replaced in an instant by determined smiles on the part of my brother and his wife and a wary look on Will's. They were concerned, it appeared, about *me*. The effect on me of what they called the 'ordeal' ahead had been the subject of that heads-together discussion. Horrible sights were what they were afraid of, glimpses of the charnel house. One or all of them should go with me. They seemed to believe my life had been sheltered and perhaps it had been, compared to theirs.

'I shan't be going into the caves,' I said as I ordered my breakfast. 'It will be some impersonal office with everything spread out and labelled, I expect, like in a museum.'

'But you'll be alone.'

'Not really. I shall know you're only a few miles away, waiting for me.'

The table was bare except for their coffee cups. None of them had eaten a thing. My rolls arrived and butter and jam, my fruit and fruit juice. I suddenly felt unusually hungry.

'Let's see,' I said, 'what shall we do for the rest of the day? We could take the boat to Formentor for lunch or drive to Lluc. This evening, don't forget, we're having dinner at the Parador de Golondro. Have we booked a table?'

'I'm sorry, Petra, I'm afraid I forgot to do that,' Piers said.

'Could you do it while I'm out?' A little fear struck me. I was going to say I don't know why it did, but I do know. 'You *will* all be here when I get back, won't you?'

Rosario's voice sounded unlike her. I had never heard bitterness in it before. 'Where should we go?'

The car came for me promptly at ten. The driver turned immediately inland and from the road, just before he took the turn for Muralla, I had a sudden bold sight of the *Casita*, glimpsed as it can be between the parting of the hills. It seemed a deeper brighter colour, a ochreish gold, an effect either of new paint or of the sun. But when does the sun not shine? The yellow hills, with their tapestry stitches of grey and dark green, slipped closed again like sliding panels and the house withdrew behind them.

I was right about what awaited me at Muralla, a new office building made of that whitish grainy concrete, which has defaced the Mediterranean and is like nothing so much as blocks of cheap ice-cream. Inside, in what I am sure they call the 'atrium', was a forest of plastic greenery. There was even a small collection, in styrofoam amphorae, of plastic strawberry trees. I was led via jungle paths to a room marked *privado* and then and only then, hesitating as two more policemen joined us and a key to the room was produced, did my heart misgive me and a tiny bubble of panic run up to my throat so that I caught my breath.

They were very kind to me. They were big strong macho men enjoyably occupied in doing what nature had made them for, protecting a woman from the uglinesses of life. One of them spoke tolerable English. If I would just look at the things, look at them very carefully, think about what I had seen and then they would take me away and ask me one or two simple questions. There would be nothing unpleasant. The bones found in the cave – he apologised for their very existence. There was no need for me to see them.

'I would like to see them,' I said.

'They cannot be identified after so long.'

'I would like to see them.'

'Just as you wish,' he said with a shrug and then the door was opened.

An empty room. A place of drawers and bench tops, like a dissecting room except that all the surfaces were of light polished wood and at the windows hung blinds of pale grey vertical strips. Drawers were opened, trays lifted out and placed on the long central table. I approached it slowly, holding one of my hands clasped in the other and feeling my cold fingertips against my cold damp palm.

Spread before me were two pairs of shoes, the woman's dark blue leather with sling backs and wedge heels, the man's what we call trainers now but 'plimsolls' then or 'gym shoes'; rags, gnawed by vermin, might once have been a pair of flannel trousers, a shirt, a dress with a tiny pearl button still attached to its collar; a gold chain with pendent cross, a gold watch with bracelet and safety chain, a heavier watch with its leather strap rotted, a child's ring for a little finger, two pinhead turquoises on a gold band thin as wire.

I looked at it all. I looked with indifference but a pretence of care for the sake of those onlookers. The collection of bones was too pitiful to be obscene. Surely this was not all? Perhaps a few specimens only had found their way to this room. I put out my hand and lifted up one of the long bones. The man who had brought me there made a movement towards me but was checked by his superior, who stood there watching me intently. I held the bone in both my hands, feeling its dry worn deadness, grey and grainy, its long-lifeless age, and then I put it down gently.

I turned my back on the things and never looked at them again.

'I have never seen any of this before,' I said. 'It means nothing to me.'

'Are you quite sure? Would you like some time to think about it?'

'No, I am quite sure. I remember very well what my brother and my cousin were wearing.'

They listened while I described clothes that Piers and Rosario had had. I enumerated items of jewellery. There was a locket I remembered her wearing the first time we met, a picture of her mother in a gold circlet under a seed pearl lid.

'Thank you very much. You have been most helpful.'

'At least I have eliminated a possibility.' I said, knowing they would not understand.

They drove me back to Llosar. The fruit on the strawberry trees takes a year to ripen. This year's flowers, blooming now, will become the fruit of twelve months' time. And immediately it ripens they pick it for making fruit pies. I had this sudden absurd yearning to see those strawberries in the hotel garden again, to see them before the bushes were stripped. I opened the car door myself, got out and walked up to the hotel without looking back. But instead of going up the steps, I turned aside into the shady garden, the pretty garden of geometric paths and small square pools with yellow fish, the cypresses and junipers gathered in groups as if they had met and stopped to gossip. To the left of me, up in the sun, rose the terrace and beyond it was the swimming pool, but down here grew the arbutus, its white blossom gleaming and its red fruits alight, as shiny as decorations on some northern Christmas tree.

Piers and Rosario were up on the terrace. I am not sure how I knew this for I was not aware of having looked. I felt their anguished eyes on me, their dread communicated itself to me on the warm, still, expectant air. I knew everything about them, I knew how they felt now. They saw me and read into my action in coming here, in coming immediately to this garden, anger and misery and knowledge of betrayal. Of course I understood I must put an end to their anguish at once, I must go to them and leave adoration of these sweet-scented snowy flowers and strawberry fruits until another day.

But first I picked one of the fruits and put it in my mouth. Iris Harvey had been wrong. It was not tasteless, it tasted like some fresh crisp vegetable, sharp and strange. It was different, different from any other fruit I had tasted, but not unpleasant. I thought it had the kind of flavour that would grow on me. I walked up the steps to the terrace. Will was nowhere to be seen. With the courage I knew they had, their unconquered brave hearts, they were waiting for me. Decorously, even formally, dressed for that place where the other guests were in swimming costumes, they were nevertheless naked to me, their eyes full of the tragedy of long wretched misspent lives. They were holding hands.

'Petra,' Piers said. Just my name.

To have kept them longer in suspense would have been the cruellest act of my life. In the time they had been with me I had learned to speak like a human being, like someone who understands love and knows warmth.

'My dears,' I said. 'How sad you look. There's nothing wrong, is there? I've had such a stupid morning. It was a waste of time going over there. They had nothing to show me but a bundle of rags I've never seen before and some rubbishy jewellery. I don't know what they expected – that all that was something to do with you two?'

They remained there, quite still. I know about the effects of shock. But slowly the joined hands slackened and Rosario withdrew hers. I went up to each of them and kissed them gently. I sat down on the third chair at the table and smiled at them. Then I began to laugh.

'I'm sorry,' I said. 'I'm only laughing because I'm happy. Children laugh from happiness, so why not us?'

'Why not?' said Piers as if it was a new thought, as if a new world opened before him. 'Why not?'

I was remembering how long long ago I had heard my brother ask that same rhetorical question, give that odd form of assent, when Will proposed going into the *Casita* and Rosario had demurred. For a moment I saw us all as we had been, Will in his grass hat, long-legged Rosario with her polished hair, my brother eager with love. I sighed and turned the sigh to a smile.

'Now that's behind me,' I said, 'we can stay on here and have a holiday. Shall we do that?'

'Why not?' said Piers again, and this time the repetition of those words struck Rosario and me as inordinately funny and we both began to laugh as at some exquisite joke, some example of marvellous wit.

It was thus, convulsed with laughter, that we were found by Will when, having no doubt been watching from some window up above for signs of good or ill, judged the time right and safe to come out and join us.

'Did you book that table at Golondro?' I said, hoarse with laughter, weak with it.

Will shook his head. I knew he would not have, that none of them would have. 'I'll do it this minute,' he said.

'Don't be long,' I called after him. 'We're going to celebrate. I'm going to order a bottle of champagne.'

'What are we celebrating, Petra?' said Rosario.

'Oh, just that we're here together again,' I said.

They smiled at me for I was bestowing on them, on both of them, the tender look I had never given to any lover. And the feeling which inspired it was better than a lover's glance, being without self-deception, without illusion. Of course I had never been deceived. I had known, if not quite from the first, from the third day of their appearance, that they were not my brother and his wife. For one thing, a man is not operated on twice in his life for appendicitis. But even without that I would have known. My blood told me and my bones, my thirteen years with a brother I was closer to than to parent or any friend. I knew – always – they were a pair of imposters Will had found and instructed. I knew, almost from the beginning, it was a trick played on me for their gain and Will's.

But there is another way of looking at it. I have bought them and they are mine now. They have to stay, they have nowhere else to go. Isn't that what Piers meant when he said being together was the way it always would be? They are my close companions. We have nothing more to gain from each other, we have made our wills, and the death of one of us will not profit the others.

They have made me happier than I have ever been. I know what people are. I have observed them. I have proved the truth of the recluse's motto, that the onlooker sees most of the game. And I know that Piers and Rosario love me now as I love them, and dislike Will as I dislike him. No doubt they have recompensed

THE STRAWBERRY TREE

him, I don't want to know how, and I foresee a gradual loosening of whatever bond it is that links him to us. It began when I sent him back into the hotel to make that phone call, when Rosario's eyes met mine and Piers pursed his lips in a little *moue* of doubt.

Am I to end all this with a confrontation, an accusation, casting them out of my life? Am I to retreat – and this time, at my age, finally, for good – into that loneliness that would be even less acceptable than before because now I have seen what else is possible?

I have held my dear brother's bone in my hands. I have seen his clothes that time and decay have turned to rags and touched the ruin of a shoe that once encased his strong slender foot. Now I shall begin the process of forgetting him. I have a new brother and sister to be happy with for the rest of my life.

Will has come back, looking sheepish, not understanding at all what has happened, to tell us we are dining at the Parador de Golondro, the little house of desire, at nine tonight. This is the cue, of course, for some characteristic British complaining about the late hour at which the Spanish dine. Only Rosario has nothing to say, but then she is Spanish herself – or is she?

I resolve never to try to discover this, never to tease, to lay traps, attempt a catching-out. After all, I have no wish to understand the details of the conspiracy. And when the time comes I will neither listen to nor make deathbed confessions.

For I saw in their eyes just now, as I came to their table to reassure them, that they are no more deceived in me than I am in them. They know that I know and that we all, in our mutual love, can accept.

Flesh and Grass

HELEN SIMPSON

1

CHOUETTE WATCHED FROM THE TOP OF THE DUTCH DRESSER AS GEORGE THURKLE DISMEMBERED THE CARCASS. HER EYES WERE AS GLOSSY AS PEELED green grapes, and from the varnished corners of her mouth protruded tiny fangs like garlic cloves. She twitched at each blow as he beat the air from the squealing lungs.

Thurkle preferred to dissect his own carcasses whenever possible, holding a low opinion of the skill of all butchers this side of the Channel. They could not tell their skirt from their brisket, he sneered, and the way they trimmed their meat was a disgrace. They had no respect for the positioning of fat seams, they stretched the flesh into clumsy rolled joints without first stripping it of membrane and gristle so that of *course* it buckled into grotesque shapes within ten minutes of meeting a fast oven. As for trying to order escalopes cut on the bias: pigs might fly.

The head and trotters were already in the cherrywood saloir out in the shed, while the scooped brains were simmering in salted milk. These were promised to Growcott, but the ears were for himself; he tightened his teeth at the thought of the cartilaginous flaps fried in breadcrumbs.

The cleaver flashed with clockwork regularity, and soon the larger brine crock, too, was almost full. Chouette stared hard at the plate holding the lustrous red-brown spleen. She was the first to hear Felix Growcott's gravel-crunching footsteps, and as he opened the kitchen door she streaked out off across the garden with the kidnapped spleen trailing in triumph from her jaws.

Thurkle rolled curses like phlegm in the back of his throat and his blue-jawed face grew livid. Then, still holding the cleaver, he hurtled past Growcott, baying for blood. Chouette ascended the Monkey Puzzle tree in a matter of seconds but lost the spleen to a prickly bottle-green branch halfway up, where it was to sway in the wind for several days, pecked at by crows.

'I'll swing for that cat,' said Thurkle, back in the kitchen.

'You shouldn't let things like that get under your skin. Bad for the blood pressure. Well, it doesn't look like there's much left of Pride, I must say. Not too late, am I?'

'No, you're just in time. You can do some filleting, then peel off the caul from the guts so I can make *crépinettes* this week.'

George Thurkle was the chef-proprietor of Barwell's discreetly famous restaurant, Chez Thurkle, much lauded by the good food guides.

'Right you are. I'll just scrub up.' And Growcott, who had already rolled his sleeves to the elbow, proceeded to wash his hands and forearms with the ebullient gaiety of a surgeon. He was a good cook, unsqueamish, pernickety, meticulously patient in his treatment of fiddly innards and membranes.

The two men stood at opposite sides of the table, slicing and chopping, scarlet to the wrists, sliding their blades across connective silverskin, through coarse-grained flesh, around bluish glistening knobs of bone, the while discussing the merits of a pig's-head sabodet sausage as against those of a well-made *fromage de tête*.

'Once you've simmered the head for eight hours, you pick it over, then chuck out the bones and teeth,' said Thurkle. 'That takes a while, of course.'

'I've seen brawn where the tongue was left whole,' said Growcott with interest, 'while the rest of the diced meat sat in jelly around it.'

'Joy should be ready for slaughter by November,' said Thurkle. 'I thought I'd save *hers* for that Corpus Christi boar's head recipe at Christmas.'

'*Sow's* head.'

They washed their hands together at the kitchen sink in a lather of pink bubbles, then Thurkle pulled the cork from a bottle of Muscadet.

'What do you think of this?' he asked, swishing a mouthful round West Wind cheeks. 'It's only last year's. I'm not sure.'

'I don't know, I think it's quite good. A little green, perhaps, a little youthfully gauche,' smirked Growcott, 'but none the worse for that.' Through the window he could see Chouette clearing a patch in the sorrel bed. She looked around over both shoulders, and assumed a tiptoed crouching position. For a few tense seconds she hunched there as though pretending to think of something else, then briefly inspected the result before kicking a pile of earth over it with busy modesty.

'The dung of meat-eaters makes horrible compost,' observed Growcott. 'It doesn't rot into the earth like herbivorous turds. That's a thought. Perhaps I could get my sanctimonious daughter Bryony to do something useful at last, insist that she relieve herself in the garden. Preferably by the rose bushes. I tell you, I'm sick to the back teeth of her holier-than-thouism.'

'Women,' said Thurkle. 'Talking of which, how's your latest? Met her at the other end of your stethoscope, did you?'

'Absolutely not,' said Growcott sharply. 'More than my job's worth. Can't afford to mix business with pleasure, old chap.' Not even Thurkle knew that he had come to this god-forsaken village of Barwell, out in the back of beyond, the best part of three hours from London, in order to escape a silly fuss about nothing which was nobody's business but his own, which had lost him his consultancy at St Pancras and – almost – his right to practise as a doctor at all.

'No harm in looking though, is there. What about Bob Lester's daughter, what's her name, the one with asthma, Marianne?'

'That was two years ago. It never came to anything. She'd been off my books for months. As I said, it doesn't do to mix business with pleasure in my line of work.'

Had Delphine had another attack of conscience? Surely she wouldn't be stupid enough to rock the boat after all this time. No. Delphine Thurkle's Hell-Hath-No-Fury quotient was the lowest he'd ever encountered, he'd say that for her. He could hardly believe how thoroughly she'd gone to seed. He remembered the crabbing of the skin around her eyes when he had last seen her, so that when she tipped her face down it formed criss-crossed pockets of pathos just like an apple after a fortnight in the fruit bowl. Still, there was nothing like fighting fire with fire.

'How's the wife, anyway?' he asked with a touch of belligerence. 'How's *la belle* Delphine?'

'Fatter than ever,' said Thurkle. 'She must weigh as much as Joy. God knows what size she'll be by the time she's forty.'

'Let's take a look at Joy,' suggested the doctor.

They carried their glasses outside, down to the orchard at the bottom of the long vegetable garden. Just before the orchard gate, a little apart from the rabbit hutches and wooden sheds and the small stone smoke-house (built to Thurkle's own specifications eight years ago by local bad boy Roger Saddington who had since worked, occasionally, as farm labourer, grave-digger, supermarket shelf-stacker and cutter of grass before finding his true métier at the nearby abbatoir), stood the pig sty.

The pig was lying on her side in the straw, gloating in the September sun. A copper-coloured Tamworth sow, she struggled to her trotters at their approach and stepped over towards them, porcine lack of ankle movement giving her the fussy straight-legged gait of a woman in four-inch heels. On each of her front trotters was the tiny hole edged with six small tattoo-like circles nicknamed the devil's clawmarks (it was through these holes that evil spirits were said to have entered the Gadarene swine). She had little weak eyes, leaf-shaped ears fringed with sandy bristles, and her boarish snout ended in a wet-rimmed fleshy button with nostrils for eyelets. Neckless, waistless, slab-sided, deep-bellied, her seaside-postcard hindquarters terminated in a bathetic ampersand of a tail.

'She's a good size,' said Growcott respectfully.

'She'll be even better once she's finished off the last of those windfalls,' said Thurkle, jerking his head towards the orchard. 'She'll be eighteen months come November. I was thinking of switching to Camborough Blues next year, but I don't know. Tamworths are such economical feeders.'

'Your kitchen refuse disposed of gratis,' said Growcott.

Joy had in fact attained this peak of portliness not only through parsnip and potato parings but also from barleymeal, cows' colostrum, late vetches, sainfoin, rape, trefoil and the occasional mouse that strayed into her sty.

'I've got rights of pannage over Shorter's Wood for October,' continued Thurkle, 'so all those beechnuts and acorns should pile on the last few kilos.'

'It's worth it, then.'

'I've got no choice, really, have I,' said Thurkle. 'All the pork round here's factory farmed. I'm not serving that muck in my restaurant.'

This led them on to what was perhaps their favourite subject – what constituted really good bacon. While they were discussing the ideal rasher's leather-like inedible rind embedded with occasional bristles, the way its lean meat did not pull away from the fat, the way its cooked fat was gold and solid but not brittle, with unctuousness behind the stiffness, a girl of ten or eleven sidled up to the sty.

'Susan Farewell,' commented Growcott.

'What do you want,' said Thurkle.

Susan went red, and said, 'Miss Stackpole said we should look around for examples, see, because we've been doing digestion in General Science and I thought a good example would be a rabbit because we had to finish off digestion with a sort of mini-project. So I thought, rabbits, because they eat everything twice. Because grass is too tough to digest in one go. Cellulose.'

'They don't teach them English any more, you know that,' said Growcott.

'What?' said Thurkle to Susan.

'Please could I watch your rabbits for half an hour,' she muttered.

'Only if you don't touch them.'

'Because rabbits are herbivores,' she persisted. 'Where's Bryony, Dr Growcott?'

'The whereabouts of my daughter are, as usual, a mystery to me.'

'And where's the other pig?' she asked, peering around the sty.

'Just back from the abbatoir,' said Thurkle. It had in fact been Pride's carcass they had dealt with that very afternoon. He was irritated by children, and wished this one would go away. Susan's eyes stretched and grew shiny, her mouth wobbled, then she ran off.

FLESH AND GRASS

'You wouldn't think a butcher's daughter would be so sentimental,' said Growcott thoughtfully. 'Ten to one the rabbits will upset her too. They eat their own offspring, after all, as well as their own droppings.'

Back at home in his study, Growcott unlocked his filing cabinet and took out his current diary. 'Plumbaceous umbrae beneath the eyes of the youngest Goodbye Girl,' he wrote. 'Snappable arms. Little red tongue, lips like licked sweets.' He snapped the diary shut, returned it to his insurance file in a plain brown envelope, and spread out books and papers for an hour or so's work on his *Individual History of Gourmandism*, for which he had already received, and spent, a generous advance from a desperate Soho publisher staking next autumn on his promise of 'something guaranteed to get the saliva flowing.' A page from the chapter provisionally entitled 'The Vital Link: culinary/sexual identifications' fluttered to the carpet. He saw it was a passage from Killigrew's Restoration romp, and paused to reread with a fond smile. 'A girl of fifteen, smooth as satin, white as her Sunday apron, and of the first down. I'll take her with her guts in her belly, and warm her with a country dance or two, then pluck her, and lay her dry betwixt a couple of sheets; there pour into her so much oil of wit as will make her turn to a man, and stick into her heart three corns of whole love, to make her taste of what she is doing.'

Sixteen, fifteen. It was all so arbitrary.

He filed the quotation, then turned to his notes on Flesh: Various. Certain unusual examples, like alligator, emetic badger ortolans barded with well-greased vine leaves and the forceful marmot or ground-hog he had already sampled; others, like lampreys, hedgehog baked in clay, gooseneck barnacles and gelatinous sea cucumbers were treats in store. A dish of bison's hump was mentioned in one of James Fenimore Cooper's novels, but he had to admit that *that* was an utter impossibility. Gregory Gough, with whom he had drunk too much at last year's Gaudy, had boasted about the delicious casseroled bears' paws consumed during a recent press trip to China, and, nearer home, of delicate donkey sausages enjoyed in Castile. For some reason the image of Delphine's cat gliding through the grass appeared before his eyes.

All he had under Cat so far was a batty paragraph from William Salmon: 'Its flesh is not usually eaten, yet in some Countries it is accounted an excellent Dish, but the Brain is said to be poisonous, causing madness, stupidity, and loss of memory, which is cured only by vomiting, and taking musk in Wine. The Flesh applied easeth the pain of Haemorrhoids.'

2

Outside, the air was elephant-coloured, packed with rain. Valerie Farewell pushed her palms into the small of her back and lifted her chin so that her throat made the little hump-backed bridge found on willow pattern teacups. Her hair was tied back with a glass cloth, and she wore a green bib-fronted apron. The skin of her bare legs had a late summer dustiness, sand-textured, with several puce-coloured flea bites around the ankles. The kitchen was clean now, and she tiptoed over wet lino to check the baby.

He was lying on his back in the Moses basket observing one of his hands, turning his fingers in the air as slowly as a rock pool creature underwater. When he saw her he smiled and started moving like a grounded sprinter, his arms and legs working, piston-like, at top speed.

Thomas appeared at the door glittering with rain and said, 'How's the little buster?'

'Come and see,' said Valerie, 'but watch the floor, I've just washed it.'

'He's cheerful, isn't he,' commented Thomas as the baby shone a broad enchanted smile at him.

'He's got a face like a daisy,' crooned Valerie. '*Look* at that face. How can anyone believe in original sin?'

They stood and hugged, then she turned and dragged her index finger over his eyebrows, pushing it backwards and forwards across the hairs, feeling the way they grew like fur.

'Well?' she said. 'Give me the gossip. I haven't been out all day.'

'First thing this morning I called on George Thurkle with a delivery and we got talking. He's still very keen on the wild boar idea but I'd have to put up five thousand and that's just to start with.'

'Another loan,' said Valerie.

'He's promised that Delphine would run the mail-order side of it.'

'Has he indeed,' said Valerie. 'I wonder if Delphine knows that.'

'I saw Dr Growcott in Stokeridge, helping some woman out of his flash new car.'

'He doesn't give up, does he. What was she like?'

'Short skirt. Nice legs.' Thomas poured two mugs of tea, then put two more mugs out.

'Women who look good in short skirts always have short torsos and short necks,' said Valerie, smoothing her hands down the length of her own rib-cage. 'Not that *he's* anything to look at.'

'Pour us some tea, dad,' said Susan Farewell as she burst into the kitchen. 'I'm starving. We had horrible school dinner today. Melanie Caldwell was sick during maths and they let her go home early. I bet it was those smelly pasties. I want to go vegetarian.'

'Over my dead body,' said Valerie, pushing a plate of toast across to her daughter.

'You'd make *me* look a bit silly, wouldn't you, if you did that,' said Thomas, passing her the blackcurrant jam.

'That's all you care about, isn't it,' said Susan. 'What about the poor animals. Miss Stackpole read us a bit from the paper about it. It's *cruel*.'

'A great deal of what you read about in the papers *is* cruel,' said Valerie coldly. 'I read today about twenty-six people burned to death watching *Bambi* in a cinema in Barcelona. I read about the rape and strangulation of some poor girl hitch-hiking up near Thirsk where your auntie Janet lives. What are you going to do about *that*?'

'Bryony Growcott says we're living on blood money,' sniffed Susan.

'I might have known *she'd* be behind all this,' said Valerie wrathfully.

'I'm knackered,' announced Judith Farewell, joining them at the kitchen table. 'Give us some toast. Any cakes, mum?' She was a large sulky girl of seventeen.

'Here's your tea. You've got to stay off the cakes until you get down to eleven stone, you know that. And aren't you going to ask how William is? He *is* your baby.'

'As if I could forget. Give me a break for a minute, will you? I'm only just back from school, and I've got to go off for a bleeding intonation lesson with Delphine at six.'

'Don't swear, kiddo,' said Thomas. 'It upsets your old dad.'

'Old,' said Judith bitterly. 'You both look a bleeding sight younger than I do these days.'

'Now he's crying,' clucked Valerie. 'Susan, go upstairs and do your homework, sweetie, then you'll be able to eat with us in front of *Appointment with Death* at eight o'clock. It's the second to last part.'

'What's for dinner?' said Susan suspiciously. 'I want cheese.'

'For God's sake,' said Valerie.

'Give us a kiss,' said Thomas. Susan went and sat on his lap and burst into tears.

'Sing a song of sixpence, a pocket full of rye,' bawled Valerie over the baby's howling, 'four-and-twenty blackbirds baked in a pie.'

'Any of that Brie left, mum?' asked Judith. 'I'm glad I'm not pregnant any more, everyone going on about safe food. Couldn't hardly eat *anything*.'

'When dow-own came a blackbird and pecked off her nose! You feed William before you eat anything else,' said Valerie, lowering the baby on to her lap. Resentfully Judith unbuttoned her school blouse and hoiked out a breast like a wheel of Camembert, its large brown nipple complete with tear-shaped milk drop. The baby latched on and Judith winced, then sagged and stared at the tablecloth as moodily as a mariner gazing out to sea.

'And when you've finished, make sure you pump enough off for half a bottle before you go to Mrs Thurkle's,' said Valerie. 'He'll need a top up before you get back.'

'When are you going to get this plait cut off,' said Thomas, stroking Susan's hair. She was curled against his shoulder, sucking her thumb.

'Never,' she said indistinctly. Her hair was cut very short, except for some hundred or so hairs at the nape of the neck which had been tightly braided into a skinny six-inch-long pigtail. 'Everyone in my class tried to grow one, but mine was the best.'

Chouette lounged in front of the fire in Delphine Thurkle's stuffy sitting room, arched backwards like one of the wasp-waisted bull-dancers of Knossos. Her long paws were as soft as rabbit's feet, the transparent quill-like claws sheathed in their individual holders. She stretched and her toes came apart like stars. Judith Farewell sat in a sullen heap beside her, a mountain crouching on a footstool, toasting her left face.

'Your turn to read, Bryony,' said Delphine from her armchair, 'and remember for that vowel sound you find so difficult, push your mouth into a little circle and then say eeeee.'

'*Sur les ormeaux du bord du chemin, tout couverts de poussière blanche,*' read Bryony, 'oh, God, this is so boring, Delphine, do we *have* to do Daudet?'

'I don't think Daudet is boring,' twittered Delphine, 'do you, Judith? But we can always try some Maupassant if you prefer.'

'Not that sexist pig,' said Bryony.

'Daudet's all right,' grunted Judith.

Chouette sat up and scratched her neck with rapid ferocity, leaning into it with rapture. Her fur flaked into ruffs like a shaggy bronze-coloured Chinese chrysanthemum. Then she started washing, raising a rigid chicken leg at the back, making dabs and darts at her hind hips.

'How's she getting on with that vegetarian cat food?' asked Bryony.

'Well, I did try but she left it, she wouldn't eat even a little bit,' said Delphine defensively. 'She likes her normal beef-and-kidney Whiskas.'

'She'd change if you let her,' said Bryony with contempt. 'You just need to keep trying. Degrading animals into pets is bad enough, but feeding them on other animals is disgusting.'

'I *love* Chouette,' said Delphine. 'Here, poospoos.' The cat gave a chirrup before jumping on to her lap and starting to knead and suckle at a fold of cardigan in the crook of her elbow.

'Baby,' crooned Delphine.

'Your trouble is,' said Bryony, 'you're just using her as a child substitute.'

'That may be so,' said Delphine. 'But I love my cat and she makes me happy, we help each other and we don't do any harm.' She yawned, showing an impressive mouthful of fillings, then leaned over and turned the fire down a fraction.

'Pass the biscuits,' said Judith, draining her mug of hot chocolate. Delphine did so, first digging into the box herself. Her passion for Mars Bars and her preference for white over red meat, for childish pap over anything remotely sour, strange or outlandish, incited deep contempt in George Thurkle. He did not allow her near the kitchen. She had to heat up her tins of ravioli and mugs of milky Ovaltine on an electric ring behind a screen in her little sitting room. Once, early on in the marriage, he had presented her with a glass of Ribena and a glass of Chablis, asking which she liked best. How he had sneered, but with apparent delight too, when she had chosen the sweet purple drink. This no longer rankled, for she had lost whatever pride she had once possessed. Now she concentrated on resignation, forgiveness and a long purgative session at Confession every ten days or so.

The cat purred like a lawnmower on Delphine's lap, stretching her neck up and giving a little sharkish smirk, urbane and smug and beatific. On the neat triangular wedge of her head all the spice-coloured stripes moved in Red Indian configuration to the central focus of her nose, which was pale pink and shaped like a half scarab. Then the cloudy third eyelids slid down, leaving her with an aspect of oracular blindness.

'*Retournons à nos moutons*,' said Delphine half-heartedly.

'*Our* sheep, you see,' said Bryony indignantly. 'Where did this assumption come from, that the animals are there for *our* benefit? It's pure speciesism, the idea that our lives are worth more than other animals'.'

'She's off again,' said Judith through a mouthful of Garibaldis.

'It's wicked,' continued Bryony. 'I met a man last summer who'd been to prison for a whole year for setting some mice free from a laboratory. He said he didn't suffer half as much as the mice would have done, so it was worth it.'

'Mice!' scoffed Judith.

'I can hardly bear to sit in the same room as you,' said Bryony frigidly, 'you with the corpses rotting inside you and all your clothes bought with the proceeds from dead bodies.'

'Bryony!' said Delphine. 'That's enough. You may think certain things but must not say them.'

'I don't care,' said Judith. 'Everyone knows she's out of her tree.'

'You must be patient,' said Delphine.

'Patient!' spat Bryony. 'You'll be telling me to do volunteer work for the RSPCA next. What's needed is action. Hit them where it hurts. We should destroy the death farms, *smash* them.'

'Hark at her,' said Judith.

'I think it is probably better to be harmed than to do harm,' said Delphine.

'Crap,' said Bryony.

Chouette jumped down and stretched in front of them all. The long fur gave her a falsely Falstaffian outline, a majestic ruff, a tail like a tuba. She stalked towards the door, and they all watched her exit in her furry Jacobean trousers, the plume of fur swaying high above her mincing wave-like gait.

Once in the garden, she crouched beside a holly bush and gargled a blood-curdling chant in the back of her throat as she watched a magpie pecking around among the leaves. Her hind-quarters slewed from side to side, she shuddered with concentration, then she sprang and the bird was gripped by her peg-shaped backward-pointing incisors. There was a frantic squawking and fluttering, and behind the French windows Delphine's lesson again ground to a halt. For better purchase, Chouette punctured the bird with her long sharp canines, taking care not to sink them right in. She wanted to spin things out. But here across the lawn came running Delphine, wobbling and floundering in her fluffy slippers, tears pouring down her face, with Bryony just behind her with a bucket of water.

Chouette growled in her throat, bit deeply, and the sharp-edged carnassial molars cut past one another like scissor blades, slicing the bird until it was quiet.

3

'ALL ACROSS THOMAS FAREWELL'S HIGH STREET WINDOW,' SAID OLD MR GREENIDGE, WHOSE UNDERTAKER'S BUSINESS WAS A LITTLE FURTHER down on the same side, 'with one of them spray cans.'

'Who do *you* think done it, Constable?' asked Roger Saddington craftily, blowing the head off his pint on to Mr Greenidge's sleeve.

'I don't talk shop off duty,' said Guy Springall, who always regretted stopping by at the Blue Boar but couldn't think what else to do on a Sunday evening. Also, he had a shrewd idea about who had sprayed the words 'Pigs' and 'Filth' on the police station door two months ago, and was of the opinion that his interlocutor had a brass neck.

'I bet you know really though, eh?' said Roger, sucking up beer noisily. '"Meat is murder." That's a laugh and a half. You better arrest me now then, hadn't you, and my partner in crime here while you're at it, he's training to be a farmer like his dad, aren't you, Peter old mate?'

'Here comes the man himself,' said Peter Talbot, edging as far away from Roger as he could manage without being too obvious.

Thomas Farewell came up to the bar and ordered a pint of Badgers. He looked around him and wondered, as he often did now, whether it was one of these men who had made him so early a grandfather.

'You got that paint off your window yet,' laughed Roger. Thomas gave him a level stare.

'Tell your mother that the Cumberland sausages she ordered are in, will you,' he said, 'when you get home.' Roger grunted, scowled, subsided.

'I meant to ask you next time I saw you,' piped up Mr Greenidge, 'when's it going to be safe to eat proper meat again? The wife won't buy owt but chicken with all this stuff in the papers.'

Thomas caught Peter Talbot's eye, then cleared his throat.

'Talking of mad cows,' muttered Roger, 'we all know who done it, it was the doctor's daughter, her with the legs, *she's* always on about being vegetarian.'

'That's enough of that,' said PC Springall, not enjoying himself at all. He had hoped for a sighting of Bryony out jogging in her little shorts – he kept his eyes skinned at all times for such sightings, and they knocked the breath out of him when they happened.

'A little known fact is,' said Mr Greenidge, 'that vegetarianism caused the Indian Mutiny.'

'You remember, I suppose,' said Roger.

'We gave out new cartridge-loading rifles,' continued Mr Greenidge, ignoring him, 'and the natives said it was against their religion to bite on animal fat, because they had to bite the tops off of the cartridges before loading, see, and the cartridges were greased with fat. But we didn't take a blind bit of notice and next thing you know there was the Black Hole of Calcutta and the Lord knows what else.'

'Hitler was a vegetarian,' said Peter Talbot.

'That's a lie,' said Roger angrily.

'Even before man was a farmer,' said Peter Talbot, 'he was a hunter-gatherer. It was eat or be eaten. The law of the jungle.' He gnashed his teeth perfunctorily at his audience.

'Talking of jungles,' said Mr Greenidge, 'two of the kids from Woodruff school were down in Shorter's Wood on Friday, down by the railway line, and they came across some black plastic bin-liners and when they looked inside they found bones.'

'Someone bin a bit lazy,' said Roger, 'naughty naughty. Have to have a word with the boys.'

'Not human bones, though, as it turned out,' said Mr Greenidge in a disappointed voice.

'Hello, doctor,' said Roger, 'we were just talking about mad cows.'

'A pint of best,' said Growcott. 'Were you indeed? And a cheese and tomato sandwich, please.'

'Have *you* gone vegetarian an' all?' said Roger.

'I just don't like taking unnecessary risks,' said Growcott. 'You and I, Roger, we both know what goes into those pies by the microwave, don't we. Snouts and lips and udders and rectums and all the bits and bobs that Mr Farewell here can't sell over the counter. Then there's the blood plasma we used to use in Casualty for quick repair jobs, anyone can buy it now to stick odd scraps of meat together and sell as stewing steak.'

'So what?' said Roger stoutly.

'Aha!' said the doctor. 'You're a braver man than I am, Gunga Din.'

'*I've* just eaten a couple of those pasties,' said Mr Greenidge.

'What's done is done,' said Growcott with his vulpine smile. 'Oh, before I forget, George Thurkle asked me to ask you if you've got any beech shavings, he needs them for his smokehouse, you know, for the hams. Usual price, he said.'

'I don't know about that,' said Mr Greenidge. 'Beech has gone up such a lot this last year, lovely quality wood of course, but if it goes on like this it'll price the better quality boxes right out of the market. Tell him I'll look in on him some time next week, see if we can't sort something out.'

'They stagger about all over the shop,' persisted Roger. 'They're in a rage. They go mental, their brains turn to sponge. Then they collapse. There's no cure. It's like AIDS.'

'You never know, Roger, you yourself may be incubating the virus this very minute,' said Growcott with something like flirtatiousness.

'You're cheerful tonight, aren't you, doc,' said Roger with resentment. He was a closet hypochondriac, and knew how even a jocular remark like this would make him worry.

After three pints at the Blue Boar, Felix Growcott went back to his study and settled down for a couple of hours of research, keeping his eyes open for any little tit-bits which might amuse George. They were meeting in Thurkle's kitchen tomorrow for their fortnightly Monday meal of exploration. He copied out a tag from Cobbett – 'To kill a hog nicely is so much a profession that it is better to pay a shilling for having it done, than to stab and hack and tear the carcass about.' Whether or not Roger Saddington would kill Joy *nicely* was a moot point. He brought a shade too much enthusiasm to his job from all accounts.

He heard the front door being unlocked, then footsteps starting up the stairs.

'Bryony,' he called.

'What?' she yelled.

'Come here. I want to talk.'

'What about,' she said, appearing at his study door, pale, lanky, severe; and he noticed as she spoke how like his own were her regular protruding teeth, markedly serrated. Ideal for scraping the flesh off artichoke leaves, he used to quip. Not any more. These days her look was enough, as they say, to curdle the milk.

'About your career as a graffiti artist.'

She said nothing.

'Just be careful,' he said. 'I know your ambition is self-martyrdom, but spray-can slogans lack the requisite dignity.'

'Anything else?'

'You'd prefer us to be purer, wouldn't you? You'd like us to practise autotrophic nutrition like the plants so that we could all live on air and water as you do. If you don't put on half a stone soon I'll have to pack you off somewhere for force feeding.'

'If there's nothing else?' she said.

'The blessed Bryony,' he shouted, enraged. 'She spreads her hands and instead of stigmata, behold! stomata.'

'I'm off out again.'

'I never should have let you stay with that friend of yours in Camden. You were only there a week, but you came back absolutely stuffed with nonsense. Where are you going?'

'To watch television with Delphine.'

'How constructive. I might have guessed you wouldn't be going out with a boy.'

'I'm getting tired of your prurient remarks,' she said, and slammed the front door behind her.

Thurkle showed Growcott a colander of brilliantly-coloured shrimp-scented sea anemones which he had obtained with great difficulty.

'Enough for *beignets de pastèques* as a starter for two,' he said triumphantly, holding them in turn under a running tap, pushing his thumb through the middle of each sea flower so that it protruded between the tentacles.

'Extraordinary primitive creatures,' said Growcott. 'Where you're shoving your thumb is both the mouth and anus.'

'Would you dry them between those tea-towels while I mix the batter,' said Thurkle.

Soon they were nibbling the stiff hot brine-flavoured parcels.

'I tried them in an omelette last time, but they looked a mess,' said Thurkle. 'Right. Next course. Your turn.'

'Lamb's kidneys,' said Growcott, 'fresh as daisies, still buried deep in their fat. I thought I'd do them trifolati, unless you've any objections.' He started snipping away at the fat and peeling off the membranes. 'Ah, that beguiling tang of uric acid. They look quite solid little things, don't they?' He raised one in the air and pinched it between finger and thumb. 'Actually, they're a honeycomb of tiny tubular nephrons.'

'Have you heard the one about the Irishman who asked his friend to pour a bottle of whiskey over his grave once he'd gone?'

'Yes. Talking of paddies, d'you think Paddy could get us another peacock if I put enough up front? Those escalopes were quite something.'

'Not a chance. He nearly got caught *last* time. They've mounted an armed guard at Postford House ever since.'

'It's about time we took another little shooting trip ourselves,' said Growcott. 'I hear they have ostriches now at that private zoo near Stokeridge.'

'Sure, Paddy, I'll do that small ting for ye, but d'ye mind if I filter it troo me kidneys first?' said Thurkle doggedly. He took a small chicken from the larder and inserted a pricked lemon into the bird's salted back orifice.

Growcott sniggered and said, 'Lemon entry, my dear Watson. The trouble with you, George, is that I've heard all your jokes a hundred times before, from a hundred other mouths, mostly at prep school.'

'Prep school!' jeered Thurkle.

'Don't knock it. All the best chefs these days are public schoolboys. That's your trouble, George. Stokeridge Comprehensive just doesn't cut the mustard.'

They spent the rest of the meal discussing farces and stuffings, helping it down with a bottle each. Thurkle claimed to have met a chef who would truss birds only with cognac-soaked string. Growcott wanted to know if he had ever tried adding the unlaid eggs to be found inside a laying spring chicken to *ragù*, claiming to have enjoyed a lasagne in Padua made with just such a gold-globuled sauce. Thurkle described how he had once helped clean and stuff a wild boar in Senlis without eviscerating it; they had made a hole under one of the shoulders, swilled it out vigorously with wine, and stuffed it through the mouth. Growcott called him a liar. Thurkle sang the praises of striped wild boar piglet with cherry sauce. Growcott sonorously enunciated, The wretched, bloody and usurping boar, pausing, fuddled, saying, 'How does it go on? Something something something about spoiling the vines, swilling warm blood like wash and making his trough in something something bosoms.'

'What *about* bosoms,' said Thurkle.

'*Bosoms?* I'm not talking about *bosoms*! I'm quoting Shakespeare, you cretin, on the subject of wild boars.'

Thurkle said, 'Good fighters, though,' and stared into his glass as if considering his own reflection.

FLESH AND GRASS

The cleaver flashed with clockwork regularity. It was bound to happen sooner or later, thought Thurkle, and at least she wouldn't be around this time to make off with some choice innard. One of his rare electric flash-storms of rage had resulted in a superhuman nippiness so that he had seized and flung the marble pestle with inspired accuracy, splitting the skull first time. Using his favourite Sabatier sharpened to a silver wafer he now removed the saddle meat, including the fillets from beneath the ribs, then cut the meat from the thighs, snipping the sinews attaching legs to torso. Strange how that little creature who used to sit so neatly hump-backed, compact as an apple, should stretch out into this shape, much like a skinned rabbit but almost as lengthy as a hare. He would use his recipe for rabbit terrine, adding extra *quatre épices* and brandy to mask any out-of-the-ordinary flavour.

Delphine would go mad when she missed her. He narrowed his eyes and snicked out the tongue. It was no bigger than a rose petal, with a patch of sharp backward-directed spines near the tip, rasp-like and dry as a piece of velcro. He wondered frivolously whether to crystallise it.

'But she has *never* not come in for the night,' said Delphine, sitting half-dressed on her bed, her face all blubbered and swollen.

'There's always a first time,' said Thurkle, undressing rapidly. He eyed her as a crow eyes carrion.

'Are you staying in my room tonight, George?' asked Delphine, amazed. They had not slept together for a year and a half. This suited her since she hated sex. In the murky past, when she was a teenager, she had found herself earning her living on the Oudezigjs Achterburgwal in Amsterdam's Rosse Buurt, standing in a window with next to nothing on, competing with other girls up and down the canal for the money of window shoppers like George Thurkle. Upstairs the light bulbs had been red for symbolic reasons, and downstairs, in the lavatories, blue, to make things difficult for those seeking to insert needles into their veins. Husband and wife hated each other, although only George admitted this fact to himself.

'Get a move on,' he said, standing beside her, naked, furry and tumescent.

'But tonight I am so upset,' she said, blowing her nose in astonishment, fresh tears oozing from her strawberry-coloured eyes.

'Over the back of the chair,' said George, who had a superstition about letting them see his face disintegrate during it.

'Your hands!' she squawked. He looked down at them; they were grained with vermilion to the wrists, the cuticles rimmed with rusty red.

'Never mind hands,' he said. He was dreadfully excited.

Sure enough he achieved ejaculation for the first time in several years, a rhythmic constriction of the genital ducts pushing sperm in a peristaltic wave from the testes to the urethra of the penis. Female sexual excitement at its peak results in peristalsis in the opposite direction, but this did not occur here since Delphine was entirely passive and trying hard to think of where her cat could have got to.

4

THE QUEUE OUTSIDE THOMAS FAREWELL'S STRETCHED SEVERAL SHOPS ALONG, AS IT ALWAYS DID IN THE WEEK BEFORE CHRISTMAS. TOWARDS ITS TAIL had formed a nattering clump of four – the undertaker's wife Mrs Greenidge and her daughter-in-law Denise, Denise's next-door neighbour Gail, and Roger's mother, old Mrs Saddington.

'I see they've caught that Thirsk rapist,' said Mrs Greenidge.

'Murderer,' Denise corrected her. 'He strangled her afterwards.'

'Horrible, horrible,' said Gail with a great shudder.

'They should castrate them,' said Mrs Saddington, 'if they're not going to hang them.'

'Only under general anaesthetic, of course,' added Mrs Greenidge hastily. She agreed with Mrs Saddington but feared the knout of Denise's more liberal views, particularly over Christmas.

'Are you getting a *fresh* bird this year?' Denise asked Gail keenly.

'I hadn't really thought about it,' said Gail. 'I suppose he'll want turkey again, he did last year. This is only our second year together,' she added apologetically for the benefit of the older women.

'You got a self-baster last year, I seem to remember,' said Denise.

'What in heaven's name is *that*,' said Mrs Saddington.

'They inject fat into the bird under the skin,' said Denise, 'so it all oozes outwards while it's roasting.'

'Not that we're meant to roast meat at all these days,' said Mrs Greenidge. 'Isn't that right, Denise? Didn't you read that roasting leads to cancer?'

'Nitrites,' said Denise darkly.

'Left to myself,' said Gail, 'I think I'd choose some of those new springy chicken nuggets. No bones, and *very* low on calories.'

'But it's all right to eat peanuts again,' Denise continued, 'the linoleic acid is good for the arteries.'

'You win some, you lose some,' said Gail.

The queue had shuffled along, and they were up near the window. Through the glass they could see Thomas Farewell in a straw boater scoring deep lines in a piece of pork belly.

'That's why I shop here,' said Mrs Saddington. 'He takes trouble. He's not too grand to sell you lights for the cat. Most of 'em now, unless you want fillet beef, they turn their noses up at you.'

Gail was grimacing at the circular display of chops with their pink-red butcher's bloom.

'I must say,' she said, 'I prefer a supermarket, it's more hygienic. Look at that rabbit hanging up over there, it's disgusting, there's blood dripping from its nose.'

'Supermarket meat is rubbish,' said Mrs Saddington majestically. 'You call that ham? It's not *ham*. It's nasty wet slices of re-moulded pig meat. Thomas Farewell still sells ham on the bone.'

'At a price,' said Mrs Greenidge.

'Modern meat's a scandal,' said Mrs Saddington. 'No fat, so it's tough as old boots. Meat should be marbled. *That's* what I'd call. self-basting.'

'There I disagree,' said Denise. 'Lean meat is healthy. We all eat too much fat.'

'Speak for yourself,' said Mrs Saddington. 'Nobody knows how to cook properly any more.'

They were inside the shop now. Against the wall on their left was a small pile of boxed eggs from Thomas Farewell's own hens, a clutch of bantams which he kept in his back garden. It was Susan Farewell's job to feed these hens, collect their eggs and date each shell carefully in pencil, since it was she who had lambasted him with Miss Stackpole's harrowing description of a battery farm: the densely packed debeaked birds; the Kill Room with automatic blades slitting throats; the efficiently vampiric Bleed Tunnel. He wouldn't put it past that woman to organise a school trip. Twenty years ago he had followed in his father's footsteps, leaving school and going into the shop. He hadn't minded it at all then, it was a good living, but middle age found him qualmish.

'A couple of nice lamb chops,' said old Mrs Saddington, nastily, so that he felt menaced behind his own counter.

On the day they broke up for Christmas, Susan Farewell had followed Bryony Growcott a quarter of a mile home before plucking up courage to stop her and hand over the Christmas present. Bryony had seemed quite pleased with it at first. It was a book about the language of plants and flowers entitled *Green Thoughts*. Susan smiled and chattered with relief as she watched her leaf through it.

'I wish *I'd* been called Bryony,' said Susan, 'or Viola or something interesting like that. Your name's in there, Bryony.'

Bryony, turning to B, found that the plant she was named for was the famous mandrake whose root, carved into the shape of a baby, charmed women to conceive; and that its dialect name in Dorset is Death Warrant, on account of its berries' extreme poisonousness. She clapped the book shut and said thank you.

'I chose it specially,' said Susan with adoration.

Some time later, at Midnight Mass at St Lawrence's, Susan stood between her parents, leaning exhaustedly against her father, nibbling the tip of her pigtail with buck teeth. His voice boomed out 'While Shepherds Watched' and made her giggle; Fear not, said He, for mighty dread had seized their troubled minds.

During the sermon she sat and stared at the medieval wall-painting which reached from chancel arch to roof timbers. It was a fourteenth-century Judgement recently rescued from a coverlet of Cromwellian lime-wash. The village children could not take their eyes off its vigorous cruelties, and while their parents directed their eyes to the vicar in his pulpit, they gazed upwards. At the top was a small dull stripe of Paradise with nothing much happening, but the remaining expanse was devoted to the torments of hell. Little naked human figures with mouths squared in howling were undergoing various stages of flaying and dismemberment. Their torturers, gleeful fiends with reptilian wings, fangs, billy-goat horns and great vulturish claws for feet, were manipulating hatchets, pincers, skewers and long spiked or hooked poles with extraordinary ingenuity. At least, their parents agreed, it kept the children quiet.

The vicar span the service out until almost two in the morning, making a real meal of it to punish them, said Susan's mother crossly afterwards, for not going the rest of the year. Judith had been snoring loudly for several hours by the time they got back, asleep in her bed beside the cot where William lay curled sucking his shrimpish thumb.

'It's funny having a tree inside our house, isn't it, dad?' said Susan as she helped him lay the table next day. 'There's the wallpaper and TV and everything safe and cosy, then we bring in this real thing from outside. D'you know what I mean?'

'Like having an open fire beside your armchair,' said Thomas, 'or some hairy great wolfhound lolloping down the stairs. I know just what you mean.'

Out in the kitchen Valerie had set Judith to cut crosses into the stumps of a green hill of sprouts. William chewed listlessly on the hem of his Activity Mat.

'You should have blanched 'em,' said Judith.

'I never can see the point of cooking vegetables just for thirty seconds,' said Valerie.

'It stops the enzymes working,' said Judith, 'keeps 'em fresher. Look at these, they're past their best, but they'd have been all right if you'd blanched 'em.'

'You just make it up to annoy me. Biology A level indeed. I don't know why you couldn't do something useful, like another language.'

'What you don't realise is that fruit and veg carry on breathing right up till you eat them if they're not cooked. Better not tell Susan or she'll starve.'

'It's just a phase,' said Valerie tightly. Susan had refused to eat with the rest of the family for the last three weeks. She had taken over half a shelf in the pantry on which she had arranged coffee jars filled with variously coloured pulses – silvery marrowfat peas, lentils, jade green flageolet, pinto and black-eyed beans – as well as a dozen tins of macaroni cheese.

There were three separate Christmas dinners at the Farewells that year. First there was Susan's plate of beans, dangerously crunchy because she was inexpert at cooking them (or anything else) as yet. Then there was William Farewell's Hawaiian Treat, an instant mush of pineapple and rice administered to him in his high chair by Valerie, the teaspoon clattering occasionally against the silvered edges of the two little headstones which had emerged concurrently from the middle of his bottom gum ten days before. Last of all there was the turkey, carefully roasted and relaxed, bulky as a brown-paper parcel, half its broad breast laid bare by Thomas's carving knife.

Susan started to sniff as Judith began gnawing its left femur.

'Oh, pack it in,' said Judith, her mouth full, indignant.

'It's a dead body,' whimpered Susan. 'It's cruel.'

'It's free range,' said Thomas.

'How can you be a butcher, dad?' wept Susan. 'I *love* you.'

'Susan, if you don't behave yourself, you'll have to go to your room,' said Valerie. 'You're spoiling it for the rest of us.'

'Cheer up, kiddo,' said Thomas, wiping Susan's face with his handkerchief. 'Blow your nose and give us a smile.'

FLESH AND GRASS

Roger Saddington was sulking. He hated Christmas. His mother told him off all day long for blowing his nose, belching (however quietly), even for sucking his thumb, and wouldn't let him escape to his room. He ached to get at the Harley Davidson pictures in this month's *Valhalla*, which was lying hidden under the carpet by the chest of drawers. He still hadn't forgiven her for making him stand still in the bath last week while she scrubbed him down. He had skipped his usual wash at work and come back scarlet to the elbows, his hair and even his eyelashes beaded with blood, hoping to horrify the schoolkids on their way home.

'I'll tan the hide off you,' she had yelled. 'Get up those stairs this minute.' She'd worked away at his tattooes with real fury, the Reaper and the wreathed skulls on his bristly forearms. She wouldn't let him out to the Blue Boar till Boxing Day. He brightened at the thought of a pub. Maybe he'd go a bit further afield, take the bike out to the Eagle and Child or beyond, somewhere he wasn't known, and pack that pig's eyeball he'd been saving in his bait box under the bed. People stood back when you chucked an eyeball on to the bar. You could see them thinking, 'I'd better watch out for him.'

'Sit up straight,' said old Mrs Saddington, bringing in the pudding with its bit of plastic holly and the jug of Bird's Eye custard. 'It's the Queen's speech.' Mrs Saddington was not really that old at seventy-one, but she looked older than she was. She never smiled. Roger was her only child, born to her surprise and horror when she was forty-three. As they said in the village, she ruled him with a rod of iron: which was just as well.

In the little flat above Barwell's police station, Guy Springall removed the frozen chicken from its plastic bag then tried to dry it off with the tea towel. Back in Matlock his parents had gone down with mumps, and since at the age of twenty-two he was still footloose if not fancy-free, he had volunteered for maximum Christmas overtime. Unable to find a suitable tin, unaware that the giblets still filled the central cavity, he turned the oven on and rolled the naked bird on to a barred shelf. He had not tried anything more adventurous than boil-in-a-bag before this, but felt duty-bound to 'eat a proper meal' after the wheezed imperative pathos of his mother's cancellation phone call. While he sat reading *Watership Down* and wishing the chicken would be ready soon since he was starving, the imperfectly thawed bird sat and seethed with saprophytic bacteria. After three-quarters of an hour he decided it was brown enough to eat, and tucked in. He had forgotten about vegetables so he ate most of the chicken, mopping up its salmonella-rich juices with what was left of the bread. Then he lay down for a nap, hoping to kill off the rest of the afternoon in dreaming about Bryony Growcott.

Bryony sat in stern silence, for her father was at his most savagely mirthful. George Thurkle was cutting slices of the *terrine de lapin* with which they were to start the meal, while Dr Growcott continued with his résumé of what was about to happen to it.

'As you know, your stomach has very strong muscular walls which squeeze in and out and churn the food up with enzymes and mucus,' he said. 'Then its sphincter opens and dumps the churned-up chyme into the duodenum.' Delphine blinked and smiled politely. Growcott took another swig of Chablis. Thurkle indicated that they were to start; with a rare fond feline smile he watched his wife spread paté on toast and eat.

'And of course, once it's down in the old duodenum, your *pauvre petit lapin* finally hops it into the bloodstream,' said Growcott. 'Delicious, George. Stronger than usual? Because by this time it's been broken down into teeny-weeny little molecules which are finished off in eensy-teensy pits in the intestinal wall called the crypts of Lieberkühn. Good name, eh? Sounds like a Gothic horror story. Then, whoosh into the bloodstream, off to the liver, and before you know it this little bunny rabbit has become part of *you*. Anything wrong, Bryony? You're looking a bit green round the gills.'

'You are what you eat,' grinned Thurkle. 'I've got some lovely seaweed-eating lamb coming in spring from North Ronaldsay, and I can guarantee I won't have to add any salt.'

For the main course, Thurkle had boiled, salted, deboned, spiced and glazed his last sow's head, splitting it except for the skin at the top, removing the eyes, ears, snout and bone at the back, then remodelling it with prunes for the eyes, celery for the tusks and a Cox's Orange Pippin between its jaws. Delphine looked worriedly at Bryony, who stared at her plate.

'Good man!' crowed Growcott. 'You did it after all. Chestnuts and spätzle too. I must say I went right off turkey after reading that an enraged *dindon* nipped off Boileau's old man when he was only knee high to a grasshopper. That's why he wrote such nasty stuff about women, did you know that,' he added, turning to Delphine with mock courtesy.

'Have you found out anything about *human* flesh in the course of your researches?' enquired Thurkle, slightly slurred.

'Supposed to taste like pork, isn't it,' said Growcott meditatively. 'Much the same consistency. There is that famous passage in *Candide*, of course, where some Turks under siege feed on the buttocks sliced from their Christian lady hostages. You'll remember that, Delphine. One poor lady complains later of the discomfort of riding horseback.'

'How did they cook them?' persisted Thurkle.

'It doesn't say.'

'I should have thought cassoulet, wouldn't you, with more beans than usual. Or sausages.'

'Actually, the thick part of the arms is supposed to be the best bit.'

Bryony stood up, turned her glass over and left the room.

'A bloodless creature, my daughter,' commented Growcott. Delphine muttered something and waddled off in pursuit. Growcott reached for another bottle.

'Absent friends,' he said, raising his glass.

'Absent friends,' purred Thurkle, eyeing the empty terrine on the sideboard.

5

'WHAT SEEMS TO BE THE MATTER, MRS SADDINGTON,' SAID DR GROWCOTT.
'YOU'RE THE DOCTOR, DOCTOR. YOU TELL ME,' she said. He almost yawned in her face at this old chestnut, which he must have heard several thousand times in the course of his professional life.

The New Year had limped in with its usual quota of Christmas casualties, unidentifiable bugs and general accidie. Guy Springall had spent several days in Stokeridge General with food poisoning, and a little later so had Susan Farewell. Growcott savoured for a moment the picture of her chalky face, green-tinged as an arum lily, with the little plait lying like a yellow worm on the pillow by her neck.

After Mrs Saddington and her swollen legs came the last appointment of the day, Mr Greenidge. He was unlucky enough to find the doctor at his most gleefully bored, for boredom produced in Growcott a puckish sense of humour, keen and humiliating.

'How are your bowels, Mr Greenidge?' he carolled, adjusting the Venetian blinds. 'Have you *been* today?' Mr Greenidge's real trouble was high blood pressure produced by obesity, twenty a day and no exercise. It was a waste of time telling him this, so Dr Growcott decided to while away the time by taking his temperature in the French manner, *à derrière*.

'Trousers down,' he smiled merrily, shaking the thermometer.

'Do I have to, doctor?' said Mr Greenidge in horror.

'Rectal temperatures are more accurate than oral ones,' grinned Growcott, thinking, *he* won't be back in a hurry. It was by this method, of course, that things had got off the ground with Delphine. She hadn't been nearly so fat in those days and when she had come to his surgery for advice, solicitous about her liver in that quaint continental way, he had been curious to see what *her* derrière looked like. One thing had led to another, but it had only lasted a week or two. It had meant absolutely nothing to either of them. It hadn't even been embarrassing to meet since. Ideal, really, curiosity satisfied and old George none the wiser. Now if only that silly little mare he was entangled with at the moment would be as reasonable.

Once Mr Greenidge had shuffled off home, Growcott drove through dripping leafy lanes until he reached the Thackstead roundabout with its tropical hoarding for the Coral Reef Leisure Complex. He needed a session in the gym after that. As the clothes fell away, he felt cracklingly aggressive, glancing at his lean legs with their appealingly fuzzy shins, tapping the hardness of his washboard stomach, flexing a bicep to observe the egg-shaped bulge. He bounded into the gym and his warm-up routine, concentrating on the hamstrings as usual. Nothing worse than a torn hamstring.

The gym was full. All fourteen of the exercise bicycles were occupied, and that flank of the room was damp with sweat, exhalation and droplet infection. Their massed rank looked like an oddly static cavalry charge, the riders staring into the middle distance like the horsemen of the apocalypse.

Growcott performed a taxing little series of burpees on the central mat, then crouched panting while the red mist cleared from his eyes. Over on the Super Pullover he could see Roger Saddington, teeth bared, eyes screwed shut, working his latissimi dorsi and posterior deltoids to new heights. The back of Roger's singlet was marked by a cross of sweat, dark down the spine and across the shoulder blades. It was a marvel that the man could move at all with muscles like that. Growcott started on the machines, concentrating on his favourite Duo Squat, and his face while he exercised was knotted in a rictus of agony. During the comparative calm of the Tricep Extender, he watched old man Talbot flogging himself onward on the rowing machine like a galley slave. His whole head looked purple with effort, and a passage about *canard à la rouennaise* slid back into Growcott's mind from last week's reading, about how the duck is strangled in such a manner that half way through roasting its blood can be pressed out to form part of the sauce.

Thurkle slipped one end of the duodenum over the cold tap and ran water through it, marking and snipping off sections where holes appeared. He was preparing the casing for sausages, and when there were about ten yards he had enough for the seven remaining pounds of flesh lying on the table. Lean and fat went twice through the mincer, with nutmeg, lemon zest, sage and marjoram on the second turning. Then he took a large piece of fat he had saved, held it to the light and smirked at it before chopping it up into pieces the size of peas and adding it to the minced flesh.

As he approached the business of stuffing the casing with prepared mixture, a process which uniquely combined tedium with obscene suggestiveness and involved a great deal of prodding with the butt end of a wooden spoon, he went over in his mind the conversation he had had with Thomas Farewell that morning. They were losing interest in the idea of specialising in boars, turning instead to the idea of small-scale outside pig rearing. Farewell, it seemed, was being quizzed with increasing frequency by his customers as to the genealogy and wholesomeness of his meat.

'More pork?' said Growcott, appearing at the door in the roguish glow of his post-workout glory. 'You're a glutton for punishment, George. Where's it from this time? I thought Pride and Joy were long since gone.'

'We're only halfway through the pig months,' said Thurkle defensively. He had not been expecting visitors. 'You can never have too many sausages.'

'Indeed not,' laughed Growcott. 'I'll buy as many as you'll let me have. I can't eat those johnnies filled with rusk and rubbish that Farewell sells. What's that wonderful smell?'

'Tonight's special. It's a monster cassoulet – Arpajon flageolets, *confit d'oie*, chitterlings, the works. D'you fancy some now?'

'Just a small bowl then,' said Growcott greedily, and they sat down together for an early supper at the kitchen table, surrounded by the sausage-making debris.

There was a knock at the back door, and Bryony put her head round the corner.

'Where's Delphine?' she asked, ignoring her father.

'Gone back to Holland,' said Thurkle through a full mouth. 'Her mother's ill.'

'She didn't even say goodbye!' said Bryony incredulously. 'She might have told me. I was supposed to have an intonation lesson this evening.'

'It was very sudden,' said Thurkle. 'The call came in the middle of the night.'

There were two bookings for that evening which made Thurkle pause and tap his teeth with his biro. Kenward, table for two at 8.30p.m. So they were back from Provence at last. He would be summoned from the kitchen for a braggartly tête-à-tête on home-made thrush paté and watermelon jam. He scowled. And Hossenlop. Must be American. That *Gourmet* magazine piece was paying dividends.

It was while he was beating the last of the cold cubed butter into a *beurre blanc* that evening that Alan, the head waiter, appeared at his elbow.

'Table five are asking questions, Chef.'

'What sort of questions?'

'Ones I can't answer, Chef. About animals, I think.'

Thurkle swore comprehensively as he finished the sauce, then barged through the swing doors into his restaurant. Over in the corner by the ilex-green hangings sat the candlelit Hossenlops at table five. The wife was thin and leathery with pale yellow hair in a chignon and glittering hard-boiled eyes. The husband was somewhat older and fatter, a courtly and benign Bostonian in Europe.

'Excuse us, chef, for plucking you from your powerhouse of creativity,' sparkled Mrs Hossenlop, who had something of a southern drawl, 'but we had to hear it from the horse's mouth, because we couldn't find the origins on your menu anywhere.'

'Origins?' said Thurkle.

'My wife means, details about where the food originated from,' explained Mr Hossenlop.

'Take the cassoulet Colombié,' said Mrs Hossenlop.

'It's a dish from the Languedoc,' said Thurkle, 'with pork, goose, mutton, white beans. . .'

'No, no!' said Mrs Hossenlop, flashing him a halogenous smile. 'We are already fully familiar with *la cuisine du terroir*. What we want to know is, can you give us details on the meat donors?'

'The what?' said Thurkle blankly. The Hossenlops exchanged glances.

'We realise we must expect to encounter some hostility in Europe,' said Mr Hossenlop, 'but it is top priority with my wife and myself to be in possession of the facts about the life and death of any creature we intend to eat. Was it raised in a wholesome way?'

'Is its flesh free of hormones and antibiotics?' interposed Mrs Hossenlop.

'What did it eat during its life? How was it slaughtered?'

'How was it slaughtered?' said Thurkle.

'This is not mere idle curiosity, Mr Thurkle, sir,' said Mr Hossenlop. 'As well as for humane reasons, we hope to enhance our eating experience. Meat from an animal which has been slaughtered while in a state of terror is always very tough.'

Outside school hours, Bryony spent most of her time on her own, even more so now that Delphine had disappeared. Her father was forever speeding off in his new car to some assignation or other. Bryony could not drive, nor would he have lent her the car.

Instead, she stayed where she was, and read, thought, conducted a passionate correspondence of ideas (mostly about animal rights) with her friend in Camden, and went for walks in Shorter's Wood, dragging her feet through the decaying leaf mulch.

Roger Saddington was on his way to work when he saw the doctor's daughter turn off down the lane that led through the trees. Since the abbatoir lay on the other side of Shorter's Wood, he decided to take a more circuitous route than usual in order to see if he couldn't chat her up.

He moved very quietly for such a big man, and Bryony did not hear him – the trees were dripping and rustling like Victorian mourners – until he fell into step beside her. She almost shot out of her skin.

'Sorry if I made you jump,' said Roger, looking gratified.

'That's OK,' said Bryony. She was thinking fast. For a long while now she had been trying to work out how she might gain entry to the abbatoir. Preliminary examinations had only revealed what was obvious to anyone who cared to look, that its bland exterior was not identified by any sign or notice, and that it was circled by a tall brick wall surmounted by broken glass and spirals of barbed wire.

'"Meat is murder",' chuckled Roger. 'You wouldn't be so keen on the animals if you knew more about 'em.'

'What do you know that I don't?' asked Bryony, trying to catch a flirtatious tone, and succeeding at least in sounding ridiculously arch. Roger was greatly encouraged.

'Take pigs,' he said earnestly. 'They're disgusting. They squash their piglets dead on purpose, then eat them. I nearly got my arm bitten off by a sow last year.'

'Tell me more,' said Bryony, staring down at the leaves as they walked on.

'They're cannibals,' boasted Roger. 'Let them loose together and before you know it they've started eating each other's tails and on into the backs. I've seen it with my own eyes.'

'So how many men have you lost like that, down at the abbatoir?' asked Bryony with a deliberate pout, the first she'd ever tried, feeling like a mechanical parody. The odd thing was that Roger found it utterly beguiling.

'It's not a job for wimps,' he muttered, sliding an arm round her, squeezing her buttocks in turn. Bryony battled with herself not to freeze.

'Will you take me in with you?' she murmured. 'I'd love to see.'

'All right,' he said, stopping and turning to her, 'if you give us a kiss.' They were quite far into the wood now, she realised. She could feel her heart pumping hard. She wasn't sure how euphemistic his use of the word 'kiss' was, but hardened her resolve as she softened her face and mouth.

'It's a deal,' she said.

He picked her up and held her in a lascivious bear hug, pressing crotch to crotch as he poked his tongue into her mouth. She forced herself to stay limp, chilly with distaste, detached and, as she'd told herself in one or two similar situations before, essentially untouched. Then she felt astonishment as some alien heat covered her skin, causing her hips to shift above his and her tongue to flick back in sinewy reply.

'Well, well,' he said admiringly as he came up for air.

'Put me down now and show me the abbatoir,' she said, her hands pushing against his shoulders, and the blood flooded into her face. She was horrified.

He kept his promise.

Through a sanguineous mist she could make out the figures of rubber-aproned men. Those giant pincers were really stunning tongs, Roger told her. The stunned pigs, shackled by a back leg each, glided off to where the man with a knife waited; then, still writhing, their pendant bodies moved on down the line to the hot tank. 'Told you it wasn't a job for wimps,' yelled Roger proudly. His voice was puny against the clatter and clanking, the rattle of chains and hooks coupling and uncoupling, the sizzling of power hoses and, above and below all this, the constant screaming.

In the dark water of the hot tank floated dead pigs, blanched of the last of their blood, their eyes cast blankly up. The steam in this room was dense with blood, and Bryony started to retch. 'Next they knock their toenails out and pull out the guts,' said Roger, well pleased.

FLESH AND GRASS

Out in the clean quiet air of Shorter's Wood, Bryony leaned against a laurel tree and vomited. Roger watched as she wiped her mouth with some grass.

'Piggy-back time,' he said. She tried to pull away but he swung her up on to his back like a sack. They lurched off into the woods, and he was quiet for a while. Then he started again.

'Ever see pigs mate?' he enquired pleasantly over his shoulder. 'They take their time. Half an hour, sometimes, the boar's in there.' Bryony considered clawing his eyes or pulling herself up on to an overhanging branch, but he had her legs in such a firm grip round his waist that she wouldn't be able to struggle free while he was carrying her like this.

'Funny thing about the boar,' said Roger. 'About his chopper. Sorry, ladies present, but I'm too ignorant to know the posh word for it. Well, his – it – has a spiral tip, so he really does screw himself into the sow. So it's proper screwing that pigs get up to, if you take my meaning.' He laughed uproariously while Bryony stared down at the shaking dark curls on the top of his head. He laughed and laughed. Then he dropped her and she fell into the leaves. He put a foot on her stomach and started messing around with his zip. She grabbed hold of one of his shins, and, shoving the jeans leg up a few inches, sank her teeth into the back of his bristly ankle, breaking the skin, biting as hard as she could into the Achilles tendon. She had strong jaws, and he shrieked, shaking her off to check the damage.

At this, Bryony was off. She was a good runner, light, long-legged and long-winded. Roger was not. He crashed after her through the undergrowth for a while, but gave up, as she knew he must, just before the start of the lane which led back on to the High Street.

That evening, Bryony locked herself into her bedroom and crawled under the bed. There, she curled into a ball. A front tooth had been loosened by his kick and she wiggled it pensively.

FLESH AND GRASS

On reflection, she decided with surprise, the most purely shocking of all the afternoon's events had been her response to that contact of mouths.

6

VALERIE LOOPED THE THUMB AND FIRST TWO FINGERS OF HER RIGHT HAND EXPERTLY AROUND WILLIAM'S ANKLES AND LIFTED HIS LEGS IN the air.

'You've been giving him too many bananas,' she said, dabbing away expertly with damp cotton-wool.

'How do you know?' asked Judith.

'The colour. The smell. These little black threads. You really are a lazy great lump, Judith. You can't even be bothered to warm some food up for him.'

'Dad said to stop giving him Beef and Bone broth.'

'But not to stop giving him everything else,' said Valerie, her voice rising. She patted him dry with a piece of kitchen towel. He lay giggling, a foot clutched in each hand, shameless and full of fun. She peered closer.

'That looks like the start of a rash to me. Better leave it to air. You watch him while I start the lunch. And I *mean* watch him.'

Valerie crossed to the other end of the long kitchen, and started taking potatoes out of the rack.

'Can we have chips?' asked Judith.

'Susan's usually back by now,' said Valerie. She had made love the night before, but her resultant good temper was running out fast. Also, she knew she had been careless but reassured herself with the thought that she was nearly forty. 'No, we can't have chips.'

'It's Saturday!' said Judith, stirred to outrage.

'And you're thirteen stone,' said Valerie. Nearly forty or not, female and male nuclei had coalesced somewhere inside her at six minutes past one that morning, fusing into a single nucleus which soon divided itself in half again – the difference being that this time each half held an equal share of the two separate people who had contrived it – and again into half, and again. Valerie said, 'If she's not back soon she'll say she hasn't got time for lunch before the bus arrives.'

'She's struck fish fingers off her list anyway,' said Judith. '"Fish have a right to live as much as we do." "Who says they don't feel pain?"'

'When did she say that?' said Valerie, exasperated, throwing down the peeler and glaring at Judith.

'Yesterday night, when we were watching a programme on salmon farming.'

'I'm not asking her to eat salmon,' said Valerie. 'For God's sake, it's only cod! If that. If she blackballs fish fingers I don't know what I'll do.'

'Why don't you get Brown Owl to work on her,' said Judith.

'Because Brown Owl is a bloody vegan,' said Valerie. 'D'you think I haven't tried. And don't do that, it'll give him a complex.' Judith was idly flicking William's tiny penis from side to side.

'Bung us a nappy then,' she said. 'I don't want him going all over me.'

'She's not usually this late back when she stays over at Melanie's,' said Valerie, hurling a disposable through the air.

Thurkle had called round for an emergency bag of veal bones. Thomas Farewell left the shop to his two assistants while he prepared them, then took an extra ten minutes for coffee in the back room. The talk turned irresistibly to their proposed joint venture.

'It cost old Talbot a fortune to set up so now it's almost impossible for him to meet his loan payments unless he keeps the buildings going flat out every day of the year,' said Thomas. 'They say his antibiotic bills have to be seen to be believed.'

'Whereas we'd have hardly any capital costs,' said Thurkle. 'We could feed the pigs on waste, particularly if we went for Tamworths and Gloucester Old Spots. And there'd be free manure for those two fields at the back. I could branch out into air-dried hams, even.' Now that Delphine was at last well and truly out of the picture, he thought to himself, the mail-order idea would have to be rethought; probably Valerie Farewell could be persuaded to do the paperwork in her spare time.

Thomas answered the telephone. 'No, she's not here. You *know* she won't come near the shop these days. Have you rung Melanie's parents to find out when she left? Out? Well, maybe they're giving her a lift. I wouldn't start worrying yet. She's probably forgotten about the Brownie outing and gone out with Melanie instead, you know what a bird-brain she is. But give me another ring if she's not back by two.'

When Thurkle returned to his kitchen, he found Growcott waiting for him.

'Restaurant of the Week,' said Growcott, waving a folded square of newspaper. 'You're in.' Thurkle grunted and made a lunge for it, but Growcott skipped up on to a chair and read aloud.

'"That noble rodent the hare refuses to be raised in captivity. Its flesh is dark with oxygen-storing myoglobin required by the energetic muscles, so dark and pungent that it cries out for a truly butch sauce like the palate-mugging bitter chocolate Italian agrodolce or – even harder to find done well – jugged hare with purple blood sauce."'

'What is this, a restaurant review or a lecture?'

'It's a preamble,' said Growcott. 'Shut up and listen.

'"Too often now the basin of fresh blood sold with the hare is really pig's blood. If this is not stirred in over a sufficiently low heat, it will scramble and coagulate, and many chefs even in high-class joints will now substitute finely chopped foie gras. But the jugged hare I encountered at Thurkle's, a restaurant which should really clean up in Middle England's cheerless heart, was the business."'

'He must have been in a couple of weeks ago,' said Thurkle. 'I wonder if he tried the *crépinettes*.'

'"Here at last is a small-scale operation intent on authenticity, eschewing spurious sophistication, where it is possible to do some genuinely serious knife and fork work. The meat was uniformly top quality and came from a butcher who knows his stuff."'

'Thomas Farewell,' snorted Thurkle. 'He's got to be joking. But maybe he only had game. I do that myself.'

'"What Thurkle lacks in finesse, he makes up for in his lack of those culinary British vices, squeamishness and wantonly wasteful prudery. Here on the menu were testicles, an ace *fromage de tête*, some genuinely rum Philadelphia pepperpot soup (tripe with veal knuckles), and a dish of sweet cod's cheeks sliced into strips, thrillingly fresh, sautéed in butter with samphire."'

'Does he say any more about the hare?' growled Thurkle.

'Wait a minute, I'm just getting to that. The pheasant gets a mention first. He says it's a coprophile's dream, refusing to be bullied even by the brutal Cumberland sauce. He's right, you *do* let your game get very high. Remember the maggots last year? Here we are. Purple blood sauce of regal velvety splendour. . .The fleet-footed beast had not been murdered in vain. . .Oh, look, he's on to your sausages and *crépinettes* now.'

'Sausages?' said Thurkle.

'"Unlike the usual bread-filled bangers, these effortfully English sausages were spot on. The meat was finely minced, oddly pungent and yet unctuous, though the casings were pretty tough. Best of all was a frog reworking of the hamburger. . ."'

'Frog?'

'French, you bonehead, ". . .resulted in a celestial *crépinette*, a sensational bundle of chopped truffles with cubed pig's fat cooked until gelatinous, wrapped in a shawl of lacy caul fat." Then he says the puddings were a bit of a let-down – advisable to draw a veil over the iffy *Iles Flottantes* – but the cheeses were something else. "I rather overdid it with three *chèvres*, *Coulommiers* and a powerful

cone-shaped *Epoisses*, known in France as the Devil's Suppository."
Ha! I didn't know that. There's one for the collection.'
'How much does he say it came to?' asked Thurkle.
'A hundred and three pounds for two.'
'Bloody hell!'
'He says that included aperitifs and wine.'
'Even so,' said Thurkle respectfully.

When Melanie and her parents returned home that Saturday evening after a day out at Boddington Safari Park, they found a note from the Farewells on their front door mat.
'"Please ring us when you get in."' Melanie's mother read aloud. '"We were expecting Susan back in time for lunch but guess you must have taken her out with you somewhere."'
'Oh dear,' said Melanie's father.
'Tell me again what happened yesterday afternoon,' Melanie's mother said to Melanie.
'We just agreed we'd played together in the lunch hour and at break time and it would be really boring to play in the evening too,' said Melanie. 'So we said goodbye and she ran off.'
'Where?'
'I don't know. Home, I s'pose. We were outside the school gates.'
'Maybe she's run away,' said Melanie's father.
'I hope nothing's happened,' said Melanie's mother. 'I'd better ring Valerie. Oh dear.'

After the phone call, Valerie went momentarily blank on what she had just heard, while adrenalin charged around her bloodstream and her heart thumped boisterously.

'What is it?' asked Thomas.

'She didn't stay with them on Friday night,' said Valerie. 'They thought she'd gone home.'

'Oh Christ,' said Thomas. 'Oh Christ.'

'They said maybe she'd run away,' said Valerie monotonously.

'No,' said Thomas. 'You know she'd never do that.' His blood vessels had constricted making him the colour of paper, and his bowels were cold and plunging.

They rang the hospitals, then the police.

'You stay by the phone,' said Thomas. 'Judith, look after your mother.'

'Try Shorter's Wood,' said Valerie.

'Yes,' he said.

He moved methodically through the woods with stick and torch, stirring the sodden leaves, flashing the light on to oozing trunks and roots. It had been raining for hours, and everything smelt sweetly of decay. Over in the direction of the village he could see a collection of lights, and thought of the scores of families he knew, each one crouched round its own television set. It would be on the news at ten tomorrow night, he thought. Probably they would want to film Valerie making an appeal. She never cried, but would she be able to keep her voice steady?

'Susan,' he shouted, 'Susan,' but it came out as a bleat, not loud at all. The rain sighed softly all around him into the earth as he shuffled on through the mulch, and the trees made a whispering as sibilant as her name.

He went home at last at gone two in the morning. He had missed her by a couple of inches. What remained had been rolled into a disused ditch and covered with a crafty rustic duvet of twigs, fallen branches and leaf mould. He had probed methodically over the area, but his stick had slid effortlessly between her outspread fingers. Still bleating and flashing his torch he had moved away.

FLESH AND GRASS

The second night wore on, and at least this night she was properly dead. She had not entirely given up the ghost until Saturday's smallest hours. Since she had been unable to move or make any but the feeblest of noises, she had carried on bleeding slowly until consciousness left her; and her body had continued to breathe and pulse and work to staunch the wounds for some while even after that.

After the attack, her blood had carried on distributing respiratory gases and ferrying simple glucose derived from the chocolate she had eaten behind her desk lid during geography that afternoon, as well as rallying to the mouth of each lesion. Multitudinous cytoplasmic platelets stuck to the edges of her torn skin, and then to each other, and managed to plug the smallest cuts. At the sites of the larger wounds, the blood commenced its business of coagulation, weaving strands of fibrin across the gashes and so netting platelets and blood cells to form clots. It was, however, an unequal battle, and she died at last.

Her corpse made a small stir in the insect world. Ants scurried around inspecting the potential usefulness of this new presence. Worms waved their blind way towards her through the covering mulch. Not two feet from the ditch there had sprung up, as pale as a noticeboard, a crowd of achromatic mushrooms.

It was Cashelmara, Mrs Greenidge's cocker spaniel, who finally unearthed Susan's remains early on Sunday morning. He snuffed around, caught the scent, and scrabbled away in the ditch. While Mrs Greenidge was still puffing over towards him shouting, 'Dirty dog! Dirty dog! Get out of there at once,' he had the shoulder between his teeth and was tugging for dear life. When Mrs Greenidge saw what he had found, she said, 'Oh my God oh my God oh my God,' and walked backwards, clutching her throat, until she caught her foot in a tree root and sat down heavily, breaking her ankle. Then she crawled back through the wood and up to the High Street. That took her a long time because she was overweight and hysterical and passed out twice on the way, but once she got there everything was all over the village inside half an hour.

'I need some strong black coffee,' said Growcott, appearing at the door of Thurkle's kitchen at five o'clock that Sunday afternoon.

'My, my,' said Thurkle, watching him hobble to and collapse at the kitchen table. 'You *have* been in the wars. A lover's tiff, I take it?'

Growcott's left eye bloomed with the stormy magentas and indigos of a shiner in its early stages. The eyeball itself was meshed with a scarlet threadwork, fine as the legs of a moneyspider.

'You've heard the news?' said Growcott.

'About the Farewell girl? Yes. Alan couldn't resist dropping by with the gory details.'

'I was called to the house to calm down Mrs Farewell. She was completely beside herself, she'd just smashed the French windows and she was squealing fit to bust. I gave her a knockout sedative and stitched her up – she'd cut her hands on the glass – but then that stupid bitch Judith charged at me just as I was leaving, punched me in the face, kicked me in the balls and generally carried on like a banshee. She's no lightweight either these days.'

'Tough luck,' said Thurkle. 'Let's hope no lasting damage was done. Here you are, double strength with a shot of brandy. She was probably hysterical too, I suppose.'

'Stupid bitch,' said Growcott again, furious. They sat chatting over a second pot of coffee, discussing the murder and wondering whether it would affect Thurkle's business. When Guy Springall appeared at the back door with a fellow policeman in tow, they both looked up in surprise.

'Coffee, constable?' said Thurkle.

'No thank you, sir,' said Guy stiffly. 'I'm here to ask you if you'll accompany me to the station. We'd like you to answer a few questions if you would.'

'Me?' said Thurkle thickly, while Growcott sat and gaped.

'You're making a big mistake,' stammered Thurkle, 'I've got an alibi for last night. And the night before.'

'Very interesting, sir, but that's not really relevant at the moment. You may find it useful later on, of course. But just now we'd like you to help us with our enquiries concerning the disappearance of Mrs Delphine Thurkle. Your wife.'

7

'HE ALWAYS DID HAVE A FILTHY TEMPER,' SAID ALAN, WHO HAD BECOME QUITE A CELEBRITY DOWN AT THE BLUE BOAR. 'IT'S NOT THE EASIEST OF JOBS, working for a man like that.'

'Mind you, nothing's been proved yet,' said old man Talbot.

'I know what I think,' said Alan darkly.

'I'm sure we *all* consider murdering our wives at some stage or other,' said old man Talbot in tones of judicious mildness, 'but ninety-nine per cent of us manage to control ourselves.'

'And let's be fair,' said Peter Talbot, 'not speaking ill of the dead or anything, but she'd let herself go in a big way, hadn't she.'

'I bet he fed her to his pigs,' said Roger Saddington, 'like in the Mrs McKay case.'

'What goes on in that back kitchen is nobody's business,' said Alan, aggrieved. 'He makes sure the sous-chefs are out in a separate room doing all the hard work, all the peeling and chopping and beating and that, but he keeps the really juicy stuff to himself.'

'Pigs will eat anything,' continued Roger. 'They grind bones down to powder. They got the stomach of an ostrich. Even if you cut them up and do tests on their innards afterwards, you never can prove they've eaten a human. They melt it in the acid in their stomachs.'

'Delphine didn't disappear till the New Year,' observed old man Talbot, 'and to my certain knowledge you slaughtered the last of his sows yourself in November.'

'If you're going to be like that,' said Roger. 'Nit-picking. A man like him would always have access to pigs.'

'He's never-ending chopping up piles of meat, or mincing it or messing it about somehow,' said Alan. 'Over keen, if you take my meaning.'

'Haven't seen much of the good doctor lately,' said old man Talbot. 'He seems rather to have dropped out of the picture.'

'Lying low,' said Peter. 'You know what they said about him and Mrs Thurkle. There may have been nothing in it, but then again. . .'

'No smoke without fire,' said Roger, drinking deeply of his pint.

'By a man's friends,' said old man Talbot.

'Shall you know him,' finished Peter.

'Ye,' said his father. 'Or is it works? By a man's works?'

'A friend in need is a friend indeed,' said Alan solemnly, opening a bag of pork scratchings.

'Ta, since you're offering,' said Roger, groping for a handful.

'What will you have?' said Peter, as Mr Greenidge joined them at the bar.

'A pint of my usual, thanks very much.'

'And how's Mrs Greenidge?' said old man Talbot. 'Ankle on the mend, I hope.'

'She's still very shaken,' said Mr Greenidge, 'but then, that's only natural. A horrible business. Horrible.'

'Poor kid,' said Alan. 'Who'd do a thing like that. She used to be in the school rounders team with my two.'

'If there's one thing that really upsets me in my line of business, it's having to bury the kiddies,' said Mr Greenidge. 'There's something about a coffin that's only three foot six, it fair destroys me.'

'The funeral went off well at any rate,' said Alan. 'I never seen the church so packed, what with the television cameras too.'

'I've had a few suicides in my time,' said Mr Greenidge, draining his pint and ordering another, 'but I've not had to bury a body in that state before.'

'Was she like, in one piece?' asked Roger glutinously.

Mr Greenidge glared at him.

'Hanging's too good for some people,' he shouted.

FLESH AND GRASS

Denise had at last persuaded her mother-in-law to come out for a change of scene. She paused on a double yellow in front of The Constant Cuppa and helped her hobble on her crutches to a window table. By the time she came back from parking the car, there was old Mrs Saddington with her chin thrust forward conducting yet another post-mortem. Oh well, thought Denise, no real harm. Elsie did seem to need to go over it and over it.

'What I keep having nightmares about,' said Mrs Greenidge, 'is the colour of her skin. It was ghastly, like mushrooms. I thought Cashelmara had got hold of some old sheet at first, you know, it was like the colour of dirty linen.'

'Loss of blood,' nodded Mrs Saddington.

'They'll catch him, don't you worry,' said Denise, dabbing at a blob of cream on the tablecloth with her paper napkin. 'Genetic fingerprinting. It's the latest thing.'

'You're not telling me they don't do sperm tests any more,' said Mrs Saddington in her sabre-rattling voice.

'It *is* one of those, just a more advanced version,' said Denise coldly.

'So why drag fingerprints into it,' said Mrs Saddington. 'I like to call a spade a spade.'

'Who would do that to an innocent child,' said Mrs Greenidge, her eyes filling for the seventh time that day.

'Ping-pong tables and fitted carpets,' said Mrs Saddington savagely. 'That's what murderers get these days.'

'I've always met my two at the school gates,' said Denise. 'I've never let them roam around the village alone. I only hope Valerie's not blaming herself too much. She looked shocking at the funeral.'

'That husband of hers isn't looking too good either,' commented Mrs Saddington. 'At least he's back in the shop, though, trying to carry on as usual.'

'Yes, you've got to try to carry on as usual,' sniffed Mrs Greenidge.

'His meat's gone right off, even in that short time,' said Mrs Saddington. 'His heart's not in it. He sold me some mortally tough stewing steak on Tuesday. I had half a mind to take it back.'

'Poor Valerie,' said Mrs Greenidge, starting to cry. 'My husband went round to settle up the bill with Mr Farewell and he said he could hear her upstairs howling like an animal.'

'You can't carry on like that,' said Mrs Saddington disapprovingly. 'Life must go on.'

'Yes, life must go on,' said Denise. 'Come on, cheer up, mum, how about a slice of Black Forest gâteau?'

'You've heard they've let George Thurkle go free,' said Mrs Saddington. 'Insufficient evidence.' She pursed her lips.

'I simply can't understand that,' said Denise. 'Surely any man capable of murdering his wife is capable of murdering an innocent child. There can't be *two* murderers in a little place like Barwell.'

'It's horrible when you think about it,' said Mrs Greenidge. 'It could be anyone.'

'Well, not quite *anyone*, mum,' said Denise. 'He charges the earth for a meal, you can't get away with less than a hundred pounds for two from what I've heard, and then it's disgusting stuff when you get it. Gail knows a couple who went there for their Silver Wedding, and would you believe it, the starter was soup. Soup! You'd expect something a bit more special on your Silver Wedding, wouldn't you. It was that or some sort of messed-about paté, apparently.'

'She was such a cheerful little thing,' said Mrs Greenidge.

Felix Growcott was lying low. They stared at him if he went out with idiotic Woodentop faces, giving him that deliberate blank look which failed to mask the lustful vindictiveness of the eyes. This must have been how the village crone used to feel just before they came out into the open and accused her of being the devil's dam. He avoided Thurkle's kitchen now, angrily aware that he was being tarred with the same brush. Anyway, old George had had his work cut out since his release; half the county had suddenly become very keen to eat at his establishment. Every table at Thurkle's was booked in advance for a month of Saturdays.

Also Felix was now several weeks past his publisher's deadline, and was a little concerned that if they went under, as seemed very probable, he might be sued for his unearned advance, which had long since been converted into more than a few metres of his shiny softly-purring Jaguar.

The latest package from the London Library had included a couple of corkers on the subject of pigs, and he now consulted their indexes before turning to his notes with a sigh of pleasure. Reading through his pig chapter so far, he admired as usual its blend of urbanity, recondite physiological knowledge and learning lightly worn.

Arabella was certainly his favourite Hardy heroine. He loved her practicality and the way she lectured her weedy husband not to be too hasty when it came to sticking the pig: 'the meat must be well bled and to do that he must die slow. . .I was brought up to it and I know. Every good butcher keeps un bleeding long. He ought to be up till eight or ten minutes dying, at least.' Bryony's greenery-yalleriness was simply jumping on the latest bandwagon. Only a century ago, slaughterhouses used to be natural friendly places where you went for a bit of a chat and a strengthening glass of blood as a prophylactic against tuberculosis.

The section that really interested him, though, was the passage dealing with the pig as horizontal man. Its internal organs followed the human layout almost exactly, and its heart provided replacement heart valves for humans. Its skin had bristle follicles much like human skin, and indeed he had seen it used very successfully as a temporary covering for burn patients. In addition it provided insulin for diabetics and the ever-useful heparin as a champion blood anticoagulant. This reminded him of the critical praise heaped on Thurkle's jugged hare – its regal velvety sauce – so causing his perotid gland to irrigate his mouth with saliva.

FLESH AND GRASS

One thing he did miss, and that was their fortnightly Monday meal-seminar; also the occasional dish of this or that which was usually on offer when he dropped by for a chat.

It seemed an awfully long time since he'd last enjoyed one of George's little dishes though it couldn't have been *that* long ago. Perhaps he would look in on him after all. Things must be blowing over a bit. In fact it was over a month now since he'd eaten in that back kitchen. It had been the afternoon George was making sausages, and they'd eaten some of the excellent cassoulet he had on as his special that night. Felix's mind skipped back to their Christmas dinner discussion concerning cassoulet and Voltaire's buttocks. How green the ladies had looked. He wondered idly again where Delphine had run off to. 'Plenty of beans,' he murmured aloud with a chuckle.

Then he made a horrible connection. He sat bolt upright in his chair and his eyes started out of his head. His skin turned cold, while his diaphragm contracted and plunged down into his abdominal cavity just as a runaway lift hurtles down the shaft. At the same time the muscles of his abdominal wall stiffened and the contents of his stomach – a colourful half-digested chyme of gammon, peas and tomatoes – were projected up the tunnel of his throat and out through his mouth and nostrils to splash-land on his notes. The process repeated itself for quite some while until, at last, his retching produced nothing but a thin yellow-green bile, by which time he was crouching exhausted beneath his desk.

Half a beat behind the organist, the congregation was already labouring to catch up during the first verse.

> Jesus lives! no longer now
> Can thy terrors, death, appal us;
> Jesus lives! by this we know
> Thou, O grave, canst not enthral us.
>   Alleluia

FLESH AND GRASS

It was Easter Sunday, and the Family Communion service had just started at St Lawrence's. As their parents toiled on through the hymn, the children were wriggling and craning their necks to inspect the clouds of musky hawthorn arranged with narcissi and green-tinged hooded arum lilies, and to stare at the grinning bug-eyed fiends in the Judgement painting.

Fairly near the back stood the Farewell family, keeping their eyes shyly on their hymn books, all except William who lay asleep against Valerie's shoulder. Valerie no longer looked anybody in the eye. She could not even meet her own face in the mirror now without being reminded that eyes were nothing but globes of jelly.

Mrs Saddington took her place at the lectern, adjusted her black straw hat and started to read with about as much joy in her voice, thought the vicar, as a raven. 'And there shall be no more death, neither sorrow, nor crying, neither shall there be any more pain: for the former things are passed away.' Former or form of, he thought, wondering whether to slip this linguistic squib of phenomenalism into his sermon and deciding against it. To his irritation he realised that Mrs Saddington had taken it upon herself to read on beyond his marker in this penultimate chapter of the Book of Revelation and was even now pronouncing with relish the doom and gloom stuff which he personally tried to steer clear of. 'But the fearful, and unbelieving,' she read, almost smacking her lips, 'and the abominable, and murderers, and whoremongers, and sorcerers, and idolaters, and all liars, shall have their part in the lake which burneth with fire and brimstone: which is the second death.' Certainly the congregation now appeared less sluggish than it had done, the children more interested, and her bully-boy son looked positively cowed when she took her place beside him again in the front pew. Thank goodness for Denise Greenidge, who read about the angel of the Lord rolling back the stone from the sepulchre door in the same voice she used with her children for *Charlie and the Chocolate Factory*.

He began his sermon by saying how nice it was to see the church so full on Easter Day, and how much nicer it would be to see it even half as full as this on the other Sundays of the year. 'It's very tempting to say No thank you very much to

Jesus,' he said. 'Well, we may say no, but we jolly well come back when we need him, don't we.' Even to his own ears this sounded querulous, so he hurriedly progressed to the Resurrection, pronouncing it a mystery but not a secret. He expatiated on the blood of the Paschal lamb which redeemed mankind from sin, fully aware that the materialistic cast of mind of his flock was so pronounced that fully three-quarters of them would immediately wander off mentally towards the Sunday roast. 'Now, children,' he beamed. 'You will all be receiving Easter eggs today. Can any of you tell me what the egg is a symbol of?' Matthew Greenidge suggested a hen, and Natasha Roberts said Jesus. 'Good, good,' he chided, 'but the egg is really a symbol of new life, isn't it.' He felt tired as he forged on towards the climax of the sermon.

'It is very difficult to believe that we will rise up in our own flesh on the Day of Judgement,' he said. 'All the laws of physics and biology and the rest of it say we shan't. The scientists tell us we're made up of billions and trillions of dancing atoms. These atoms arrange themselves in patterns, holding hands like ring-a-ring-of-roses to make molecules. But sometimes the dancing goes wrong and the patterns are disrupted. Then we get ill. Well, it's hard enough to believe all that, isn't it. Pull the other one, you feel like saying, or at least I know I do. So why not make the leap into Christian belief too? We shall rise up, and we must believe this, however hard it is to do so, or all the rest is nonsense.'

'It *is* nonsense,' thought Valerie, as William started to howl in her arms. Judith yawned and wondered why churchy types found the idea of death so unspeakable; you didn't exist before you were born and you didn't exist after you died, and that was that. But it was difficult to take in that Susan had vanished off, or, rather, into, the face of the earth, and she wearily took out her bundle of tissues as the tears welled up.

Thomas had not really been listening, although one or two phrases had penetrated the blankness on which he was trying very hard to concentrate. That line about rolling back the stone from the door had made him catch his breath. Grief sat inside his rib-cage like a boulder and nothing could budge it.

8

IT WAS THE MIDDLE OF APRIL AND THE SKY WAS A WATERY, WELL-RINSED BLUE. THE AIR WAS INTERESTING WITH FRESH SPRING SMELLS LOOSELY KNITTED into the chime of birds and the noise of children playing in back gardens. In the fields around the village of Barwell, lambs were performing their vertical four-point take-offs into the air, oblivious to the fact that a month later they would be lying piecemeal in clingfilm. The ability to contemplate death is an exclusively human attribute, or so we imagine.

Judith Farewell was exercising this attribute this Saturday morning, crouched at the side of her sister's grave. The white marble headstone sparkled in the sun, distressingly jaunty alongside its more weathered companions. Judith squinted into the brightness, her eyes weakened by crying, then withdrew to the nearby shade of the yew tree, where she sat on a decently adult-length tombstone and started to scratch at its dappling of jade and egg-yolk-coloured lichen. Her Biology A level was in six weeks time, and now she mutteringly rehearsed her knowledge of symbiosis, running through the lichen's mutually beneficial partnership of fungus and green algae, the fungus extracting minerals from the stone and the algae drawing nourishment from sunshine.

'I wish I hadn't been so nasty to her,' she sniffed.

She heard someone coming, and watched with hostility as Bryony Growcott advanced on Susan's grave. Bryony was carrying a bunch of flowers she had picked from the meadow which formed an extension of the school playground in summer. She had stuck these bluebells and lilies-of-the-valley in a marmalade jar filled with water. When she noticed Judith she stopped, then walked slowly over towards her, dragging her sandals in the grass.

'They'll only die in the sun,' said Judith.

'I know,' said Bryony humbly.

'What are you doing here.'

'I'm sorry. I didn't know I'd be barging in. Oh, Judith, I wasn't very kind to her.'

'Yeah, she had a thing about you, didn't she,' jeered Judith. 'Bryony this, Bryony that, we got really sick of the sound of your name.'

'I'm sorry.'

'You and your rotten father.'

'My father is not me,' said Bryony in a sudden blaze. 'If I had my way, I'd be no part of him.'

'I hate your father.'

'You're not the only one.'

'He came smarming round our house the morning they found our Susan, pretending it was to help mum, how dare he.'

'How do you mean?' said Bryony, squatting down beside Judith in the green-black shade.

'Never you mind,' muttered Judith.

They were quiet for a while, then Bryony asked, 'How *is* your mother?'

'It's awful at home,' said Judith in a rush. 'I take her a cup of tea in the mornings and she's always lying there with a wet face staring at the ceiling. Sometimes she says she thinks in her dream that it's all just a bad dream, but then she wakes up and finds it's real again. Dad gets that dream too. So do I. Sometimes she shuts herself in her room and screams. I can't stand that. It makes Dad cry too. She won't let him in.'

'Oh Judith,' said Bryony.

'She won't let go of William,' continued Judith tonelessly. 'She has him in her room at night now. She won't let me near him. He *is* my baby, you know. And Susan was his auntie.'

'Susan gave me a book about plants at Christmas,' said Bryony. 'You can have it if you want it. You're her sister.'

'Do you mean that?' asked Judith, looking at her in straight surprise.

'Of course. Come back now with me. Don't worry, Dad's out all day today. He's taken his new girlfriend to London.'

They stood up and went over together to Susan's grave. With a rough cawing and battering of wings, a small cloud of rooks ascended from the yew tree into the blue. Several of their number were shot by Paddy the poacher later that day as they flew over Shorter's Wood, and their bodies were sold the next morning to George Thurkle, who slit along their breastbones, peeled back their skin and feathers in one and baked their breasts in a parsley-and-mushroom pie which then appeared as the Tuesday Chef Recommends.

On their way back to the doctor's house, Judith and Bryony found themselves talking to each other with an intimacy which astonished both of them. Bryony said that she couldn't look at anybody now without seeing the bones inside them like X-ray lacework. Judith said she knew just what she meant, though she got it even worse because of doing Biology.

When they got in, Bryony made them some coffee, and opening the refrigerator for milk, she noticed a bottle of Bollinger in the salad compartment.

'For the girlfriend,' she said acidly. 'He calls her his little Circe. He always calls them that, can't even be bothered to change the chat-up line.' Then she seized the bottle and looked at Judith. 'Let's share it,' she said, and started peeling off the foil. Judith goggled and said, 'It's only eleven o'clock.'

'Who cares,' said Bryony, and the cork flew out on a whoosh of foam, smashing a pane of glass in the kitchen dresser.

They drank and talked and looked at Susan's plant book together. They grew flushed in the face and laughed and cried. Bryony sprawled on the sofa with her heels on the mantelpiece. Judith unbuttoned the top of her shirt and flapped it about her broad bosom for air. She looked wickedly over her hot red cheeks at Bryony.

'Fancy us getting on like this,' she said. 'What with me being your stepmother and all.'

Bryony stared.

'My what?' she said.

'You heard me,' said Judith belligerently. 'You're little William's half-sister.' She laughed as she watched Bryony's face.

'Why didn't you tell anyone?' said Bryony after a while.

'Your dad,' said Judith. 'He said if I told on him, he'd show everybody.'

'I remember the night you had William,' said Bryony slowly. 'He came early, didn't he, and fast, and they couldn't get you to Stokeridge General on time.'

'That's right,' said Judith coldly. 'So I had him in my own bed, with the midwife at one end and your lovely father at the other. That really made him feel chuffed, I bet, delivering his own kid. Yuk. He makes me sick.'

'Show everybody what?' said Bryony, returning to Judith's earlier words.

'First time I wheeled William out,' continued Judith relentlessly, 'I heard Mrs Saddington call him a little bastard and she meant me to hear. I just laughed, I thought, like father like son. Because if you must know, well, he made me go a bit mad, I think, and I can't believe it now but I thought he was really It and clever and all that. I thought he was like God. All right, I let him take dirty photos of me. What a laugh. Look at me now. I was stupid.'

'You were fifteen,' said Bryony. 'You could have got *him* into trouble.'

'Don't think I didn't think of that,' snapped Judith. 'But I couldn't face him sending the photos to dad and mum like he swore he would, and copies to the headmistress, and my stupid stupid letters to him. I'd rather have had the baby. Anyway, the law doesn't work like that, does it. He'd have wormed his way out. So I decided to put up and shut up. Still, it doesn't seem to matter so much these days.' She started to cry. 'But you won't let on, will you, Bryony? Swear you won't.'

Bryony was thinking.

'I bet that's why they got a new school doctor in,' she said. 'I bet they got some complaints. I never talk to anyone, I wouldn't know.'

'He's a dirty old man,' shouted Judith. 'Sorry, I know he's your dad, but he is.'

'I didn't know it was as bad as that,' said Bryony.

'I was even starting to think he fancied our Susan,' said Judith. 'He kept on coming round when she got food poisoning.'

'Oh please don't say any more just now,' said Bryony. 'Remember fifty per cent of me came from him. How do you think that makes me feel.'

'Maybe your mother had an affair,' said Judith consolingly. 'You never know. I mean, it's a possibility, isn't it, if you find yourself married to someone like that.'

'No,' said Bryony. 'Anyone can see I look like him. Same horrible teeth, same hair, same pointy ears.'

'Yeah,' said Judith. 'Oh well, tough cheddar. You don't have to *be* like him.'

'Listen,' said Bryony. 'I've had an idea. He's away all day. Let's see what we can find in his study. It's locked, but I know where he keeps the spare key.'

'My photos,' said Judith. 'My letters.'

'*Exactement*,' said Bryony.

That afternoon the two girls turned Felix Growcott's study upside down. Judith found what she wanted quite early on, and stood tearing it into ragged petals of paper, baring her teeth with effort and fury.

'I bet you'd make mincemeat of a telephone directory,' said Bryony respectfully, staring at the pile of confetti at Judith's feet.

'Yes, I'm strong,' said Judith grimly. 'I may be stupid, but I'm strong.'

They did not stop there. It was too interesting. Judith leafed through the typescript of the *Individual History of Gourmandism* and discovered copious marginal notes in Felix's handwriting which gave vividly informal details charting his flesh-eating experiments, including the provenance of the peacock escalopes, the risky business over the zebra importation (horsemeat indeed!), and the promise of bears' paws under plain cover from Szechuan.

'Your dad'll eat anything,' chortled Judith. 'Folks won't like it when they find out what he's been up to. They'll look to their pets, I shouldn't wonder.'

Bryony unlocked the filing cabinet, and they started riffling through the files. Judith pulled a brown paper envelope from a docket marked Insurance.

'What's this then,' she said, pulling out Felix's private catalogue of lust. They read together in shock and fascination.

'Marianne Lester,' said Bryony. 'So it was true. And Delphine! I don't believe it! Delphine!'

They could not look at each other.

'Sally Cheeseman!' said Judith. 'Well, she always *was* a bit that way. But Pauline Simmonds! Who would have thought it. It's not just me that's stupid, then.'

'And Susan,' said Bryony sorrowfully. 'You were right.'

'But he never touched her,' said Judith, scrabbling through the pages to the last entry.

'Unless,' said Bryony uncertainly.

'No,' said Judith. 'He wouldn't do that.'

'No.'

Again they could not meet each other's eyes.

'Let's make some coffee,' said Bryony.

As they crossed the hall, she noticed an envelope on the front doormat. It was addressed to Bryony and bore a Dutch postmark. Inside was a card congratulating her on her eighteenth birthday, which had fallen unmarked a week ago; also, a tiny pair of clogs painted with windmills on a silver chain, and a folded letter which they read together while the kettle boiled. Delphine had packed her bags, it emerged, on finding a plumy spice-coloured tail at the back of her husband's sock drawer. She had felt unable to carry on living with the murderer of her darling, she wrote, and knew she should have left him long ago. Now she had found a job in a bakery in Delft and was enjoying her new life. Someone had told her that she was entitled to a proportion of Thurkle's restaurant profits since she had worked for him unpaid for years, so she was also filing divorce proceedings on grounds of mental cruelty, and imagined she might be able to buy a nice little apartment in time. She hoped Bryony would visit her. She concluded, 'My advice to you on your eighteenth birthday, dear Bryony; do not vacillate. But I hardly need to say this to you, who are as fearless as a lion.'

'Huh,' said Bryony. 'I'm frightened now.'

'Don't be soft,' said Judith. 'Things are all coming together.'

'Even so,' said Bryony, 'I can't stay here any more.'

They sat hunched over their coffee mugs at the kitchen table and at last agreed on a plan of action. First they painted Tipp-Ex over the names in Felix Growcott's diary. Then they took it down to the newsagent's with certain key pages from the *Individual History of Gourmandism*, and passed a busy twenty minutes at the photocopier. Next, they let themselves into Dr Growcott's surgery and carefully sellotaped the enlarged xeroxed pages to the glass so that they were clearly legible to anyone passing his High Street window.

'Right,' said Judith. 'Let's split.'

Bryony was doubled up with a fit of the giggles, her eyes streaming.

'Don't lose your nerve now,' said Judith sternly. 'And remember, if PC Plod won't have you, come and stay with us. I'll hide you in Susan's old room.'

When Bryony explained her situation to Guy Springall, however, he was more than happy to take her in. His romanticism had caused him trouble before and would eventually lead to his being ejected from the police force, but this afternoon it came into its own. He offered her his flat, but coolly she took the key to one of the cells and locked herself in. She had left her father's house forever, she said. She had three hundred pounds in a savings account, and now needed to plan her future. Perhaps Delphine would let her stay for a while. She'd have to think about it.

9

Early on Sunday morning, Guy, who had not slept much, made some coffee and toast and took it down to Bryony's cell. She was awake, sitting on her bed with her eyes closed, face to the sunny frosted pane reinforced with chicken wire which glazed the barred window.

Guy had last night supplied her with the two pillows from his own bed and also his duvet, his boil-in-a-bag ratatouille, his only clean handkerchief and his digital alarm clock. He had looked through his bookshelves with mounting desperation for something which fitted his idea of her mood and intellect, and had finally offered his Complete Shakespeare (untouched, in mint condition). In the small hours, Bryony had turned to the early poems, unfamiliar to her, and had become engrossed in the clever eroticism of 'Venus and Adonis', reading of forceless flowers and sweet bottom grass until she was soothed and her lids drooped; her eyes crawled down the tickling stanzas as far as the hunting scene and the boy's capitulation, at which point she fell asleep, mercifully well before the climactic goring.

> Tis true, tis true, thus was Adonis slaine,
> He ran upon the Boare with his sharp speare,
> Who did not whet his teeth at him againe,
> But by a kisse thought to persuade him there.
> And nousling in his flanke the loving swine,
> Sheath'd unaware the tuske in his soft groine.

Both Bryony and Guy enjoyed lyrically sexual dreams that night, in their separate beds. Bryony in particular was surprised to feel so happy when she woke up. She couldn't remember waking before to this sense of everything being new and different and changed for the better.

Now, as they sat either side of the cell bars sipping their coffee, Guy struggled to keep himself from fatuous beaming, while Bryony, with faltering and unaccustomed openness, attempted to describe her brutal enfranchisement and the events which had led to it.

They talked for several hours without noticing the time: about Growcott's goatishness and wolfishness and whether Bryony felt he was capable of murder; about Guy's fell walking in his native Derbyshire, and his flute playing, and Bryony's ambition to visit Lundy and Lindisfarne; about their separate pasts and childhoods; about life and death and her desire to stay behind bars until she had got used to her newly descended freedom and was sure she was safe from her father.

'It's probably better if I don't know about the surgery window and the study being turned upside down,' said Guy. 'Your father would have been in by now if he thought it was a burglary. Meanwhile, I'd better deliver the diary and Mrs Thurkle's letter and so on to the powers-that-be in Thackstead and let them decide what happens next.' He left her reluctantly in order to make his delivery. She smiled, using unaccustomed muscles, beginning to look more like an eighteen-year-old girl and less like an avenging angel with every hour.

Mrs Saddington was in a horrible temper after a morning of spring-cleaning. She had undertaken this in a spirit of anger and self-righteousness. It was the fault of the sun. What had passed muster, not to mention duster, during winter now looked shamefully fly-blown in the light of April. Sepia-tinted rooms in which windows had remained clamped shut to conserve heat had been exposed as smeary fetid disgraces.

FLESH AND GRASS

Now the house stank sweetly of synthetic lavender furniture spray and the ingratiating odour of pre-vac carpet granules. She had polished the filthy brass with hatred, eighteen candlesticks which no candle had penetrated since their manufacture a hundred years ago. She had torn down the net curtains and washed them in water which turned incriminatingly funereal on contact. These were now out on the line in hang-dog rows and she was on tenter-hooks to get them back up because it so appalled her to be naked like this to the street. Meanwhile she swiped round the fur of dust on the mouldings and attacked the windows with crumpled newspaper.

Roger's room had been saved for the force of her final fury. It was the only area where she allowed him any latitude and in consequence it was an authentic hell-hole. Their agreement was that she would not enter this sanctum without permission, and he kept it locked although she knew he knew she had a duplicate key. Now, aware in some corner of her psyche that his sheets had not been changed since well before Christmas, she braced herself and entered.

The smell was quite extraordinary. Those sheets accounted for some of it, of course, and also the drifts of dirty socks and pants. The fact that he had nailed his windows up and kept the old black-out curtains drawn day and night doubtless created conditions which nourished the miasma. But there was something else this time, something extra in the torpid air. She flicked the light on. He preferred a low-watt unshaded bulb, and this shone weakly on the light-crushing purple of the walls. A brief inspection of his book case showed that he had almost doubled his reference library on torture, weight-lifting and the occult. Nothing so far on motorbikes that she could see. She put her foot down at motorbikes.

She knew his secret hiding places and went now to lift the carpet over in front of the chest of drawers. Here she found the three most recent issues of the motorbike monthly, *Valhalla*. This made her grind her teeth and swear at last; the sneaking snivelling liar, just like his father. She promised herself a violent scene tonight, and started to revel in it in her imagination as she knelt down now to examine his other hiding place, which was the bait box he kept with the fishing tackle under the bed. She reached her arm out gingerly; she didn't want another fish hook in her thumb pad. Her groping fingers closed on a moist squirming clot of maggots.

With a hoarse obscenity and a speed well-nigh incredible in a slothful woman of seventy-one, she leaped up and smeared this hand backwards and forwards across the bleary duvet cover until it was quite free of the offending coagulum. He had done this once before, when he was thirteen, stored live bait under his bed and then forgotten about it, but she thought he had learned once and for all that time (from which he had emerged half-maimed) *not* to do it. Breathing fire and brimstone she fetched rubber gloves, disinfectant and a bucket of water and returned to the bedroom. She pushed his bed back against the wall and used sheets of *Valhalla* to clear the semi-phosphorescent galaxy of larvae from the carpet. He had not bothered to seal the lid of his tupperware bait box, so of course they had escaped. There was the old tobacco tin in which he stored his fish hooks. He probably tried to hide things from her in there too. His deceit was boundless. She levered the lid off and stared. Coiled inside like a yellow worm was a skinny braid of hair. She recognised it immediately.

Within ten minutes Mrs Saddington was sitting in the Farewell's front room waiting for Valerie to come down. She hadn't needed to think twice. Once she had washed her hands and donned her dun-coloured summer coat and hat, she crossed to the Farewells in the horrible sunshine with the plait in an envelope in her pocket.

Thomas had answered the door, looking shambolic and unshaven. Inside was no better. The windows were filthy and there were vases of dead flowers everywhere, left over from the funeral. She noted the overflowing waste paper bin and the plastic toys which littered the unswept carpet. Judith sat hunched in the depths of the biggest armchair and did not bother to do more than grunt a hello before returning to her bar of fruit-and-nut and her broadsheet of Hollywood's dirty laundry.

Valerie came down at last, clutching the baby, who was pulling her front hair round over her face and practising his new trick of pinching folds of her neck between his sprouting fingernails. Even allowing for this, she looked shocking. The sun shone in and showed her blotchy pallor, her sore eyes, the way her face had fallen in round the nose-to-mouth lines.

Most uncharacteristically, Mrs Saddington quailed.

'Hello, my little man,' she said, all rusty saccharine, as Valerie lowered William to the carpet. He ignored her and beetled off on all fours towards his alpine mother.

'What can I do for you, Mrs Saddington,' said Valerie. Deep inside her floated a tiny seahorse-shaped creature, only an inch long but already with nostrils, lips, tooth-buds and a four-chambered heart; so far she had been too distracted even to suspect its existence.

'I know who done it,' said Mrs Saddington, the words very cumbersome in her mouth, aware as she spoke that they weren't grammar, but finding they emerged with an irresistible force of their own.

All three stared at her then. The baby cracked his head on a chair leg and started to scream, but they ignored him.

'I found this under the bed when I was cleaning his room,' said Mrs Saddington, taking out the envelope and holding up the plait between finger and thumb. It caught the sun. The room was very quiet.

'My own flesh and blood,' said Mrs Saddington gruffly.

'Susan,' said Thomas, and started to choke like a cat with a furball.

Valerie pounced and grabbed the plait, holding it into her as though she had stomach cramp.

'It's a terrible thing for a mother,' said Mrs Saddington, almost conversationally.

'Where is he,' said Judith. She looked huge and dark as she ascended from the armchair, and suddenly active too, so that Mrs Saddington felt a little throb of excitement.

'Up at the abbatoir.'

'Come on,' said Judith.

They left Thomas holding the baby and bleating about the police. On their way Mrs Greenidge called out to them from her garden and they stopped to tell her. She insisted on joining them and made them get into her car since she still could not walk far. Thomas meanwhile, having failed to contact Guy Springall and unable to find the telephone directory or get through to the operator, had strapped William into his buggy and was charging up the High Street with the baby screaming delightedly in front of him. When he reached the police station, however, he found it had closed its doors for the day.

At college, Guy had shared a flat for a year with a positive thinker who had blutacked a poster over the fireplace proclaiming 'Today is the First Day of the Rest of Your Life.' Now, waking on Monday, Guy remembered everything in a flash with an unclouded gladness he had not felt since early childhood and said out loud, 'Today is the Second Day of the Rest of My Life.'

It was early again, six thirty or so; he opened his bedroom window and stood shuddering with pleasure as the mist-smudged sun climbed the sky. Everything was fresh and chill and damp. He could see a row of back gardens, moist silver-bladed lawns and box hedges and cedars. In the nearest, a tabby cat was playing the fool in a flood of light, dancing at a fly. Guy even read his own naked happiness into the side wall of next door's Spar Grocery, admiring the way the sun changed its usual raw brickiness into prismatic oblongs of ginger, charcoal and ruddle.

He stayed on duty at the desk for a long and uneventful morning, visiting Bryony's cell a couple of times with cups of coffee. She had agreed to come out with him on his afternoon off; at one o'clock precisely he bolted the doors of the little police station and shot upstairs to his bedroom, out of his uniform and into his jeans. At five past one she smiled, unlocked the door to her cell, and stepped outside to his ten-year-old Beetle with its rust-fretted mud-guards.

'Very reliable,' he said, wrenching open the passenger door, which was stiff on its hinges to the point of howling, 'but not exactly very smart, I'm afraid.'

'You shouldn't run yourself down,' she said, and was astonished at this unprecedented sally into flirtatiousness on her part.

There was little traffic about that afternoon, and Guy took a route which led them through farmland. The hawthorn hedges bordering the lanes along which they drove filled the car with their river-smelling scent. Bryony sat with one elbow leaning on the open window and let her hair fall forward across her face. She closed her eyes and savoured the sensation of freedom, hoping that he would keep quiet. He drove on in silence, noticing every detail of whatever came into his view with the new pleasurable sharpness.

His favourite pub, the Sun and Whalebone, had an airy side room where food was served. They sat at a table by the open fireplace and Guy ordered a bottle of Fleurie because it was the most expensive of the six wines on the list. The stone at the back of the hearth was carved with a stag scorched black, his curves infilled with a silky silt of wood ash left over from the winter months.

'Here's to your new life,' said Guy, and they smiled at each other as each took a sip of the red.

At the same time as Guy sat toasting Bryony, the truck ferrying that week's consignment of pigs from Talbot's farm turned in at the gates of the abbatoir and drove round to the usual unloading area, closely followed by Mrs Greenidge's Hillman Imp.

The truck driver had used his security card to operate the front gates. Afterwards he told the court he had taken no notice of the overcrowded little car-load of women behind him, assuming it was full of wives or tealadies. Two abbatoir workers, Marlon Briggs and Roger Saddington, appeared to help him unload the pigs as usual. It was always a bit of a tricky job, even more so that day because it had been hot and the pigs were overcrowded and furious. They had been scrambling and climbing on top of each other to reach the air vents, biting at random, their inability to sweat causing their temperatures to soar. A couple of them had already suffocated en route. Marlon and Roger had helped prod the pigs out of the truck and down the ramp into the entrance pen, and because there were more of them than usual they had been extra crowded in there too, squealing and screaming fit to bust, scrabbling for air and taking great chopping bites at each other. Then the women had come up, one old one, one fat one, one a bit wild-looking and one on crutches, and they'd got themselves in a circle around Roger and started waving something in his face and shouting at him. He'd laughed at first, or the truck driver thought he had from his face, but he couldn't hear anything above the pigs' noise; but when he'd tried to push past them, the fat one had shoved him against the bars. He'd climbed up backwards a little way, obviously meaning to jump clear of them, and that was when the old one grabbed a crutch and used it to give him a shove in the chest. He lost his balance and next thing they knew he was in there with the pigs. That was the end of him. By the time they'd run for help and managed to sort the pigs out, he was in pieces, and was dead on arrival at Stokeridge General.

At the moment of Roger Saddington's death, Guy Springall was pouring the last of the wine into Bryony's glass.

'Say something to me in French, then,' he said. She had been telling him about her A levels. He did not yet reveal that he was himself fairly fluent in French and German thanks to his father's army career, which had meant his family had lived abroad until he was ten.

'*La plume de ma tante,*' she said, airly patronising. '*Le canif de mon frère.*' He looked hard at her. '*Vos yeux sont bruns,*' she went on, '*et vous me regardez comme un homme qui ne veut jamais parler, lui dont la langue est silente.*' There was a pause and they held each other's eyes.

'*Pas du tout,*' he said. '*Mais s'il y a beaucoup d'art à parler, il n'y en a pas moins à se taire.*'

She laughed out loud in surprise.

The waitress appeared again and asked for their order with undisguised impatience. They consulted the felt-tipped menu.

'Mushroom terrine,' said Bryony.

'Finished,' said the waitress, who was fifteen and knew nothing yet of servility. 'You should have ordered before. You could have chatted while you waited then.'

'What's left?' asked Guy.

'Everything's finished now except lamb chops with spring veg,' said the waitress.

'All right,' said Bryony. 'Let's have that.' She felt her stomach heave.

'Coming right up,' sang the waitress, and bounced off to the kitchen. She couldn't wait to go down to the river, and hopped around impatiently while her mother assembled the two plates of food.

'Are you sure?' said Guy. 'Don't feel you have to because of me. Don't compromise your principles.'

'Don't dare talk to *me* about principles,' said Bryony crossly, 'you policeman you.'

'Why, then?' he asked.

She did not answer. She did not know the reason herself.

'I ought to be as miserable as sin,' she said after a while. 'But I'm not. At least, not all the time.'

'Good,' said Guy, nonplussed.

The waitress arrived and unloaded her tray. Bryony and Guy stared at the trim rosy cutlets with their side plates of carrots, new potatoes and peas.

'Mint sauce?' asked the waitress, teaspoon poised.

'No thanks,' they said in unison. She left them to it. 'Oh go on,' said her mother resignedly, 'off you go and enjoy yourself.'

'I still don't understand,' said Guy. 'Why?'

'That's my business, isn't it,' said Bryony. She took a deep breath and picked up her knife and fork.

EPILOGUE

THE TROUBLE WITH THIS SORT OF STORY IS THAT IT MAKES A PILE-DRIVING DEMAND FOR A SCAPEGOAT. SOMEONE MUST BE TO BLAME SO THE REST can be absolved, even though the true villain is, of course, that figure on the horizon with the unselfing scythe slung over his shoulder. Not much can be said in Roger Saddington's defence except that he performed the function of Reaper's Rep fairly and squarely, with altogether more swagger than either George Thurkle or Felix Growcott could have managed. Most things grow easier with practice, and he had been used to being paid a respectable weekly wage for slaughter; as the Judge said, he obviously did not know where to draw the line.

Old Mrs Saddington was found guilty of manslaughter. She was sentenced to five years in prison where she found there were indeed ping-pong tables and, in certain areas, fitted carpets. She curses her son daily and has come to see herself as the instrument of divine retribution. She is not a popular prisoner.

George Thurkle continued to prosper until the cat got out of the bag. From then on he was held in such universal abhorrence that he had to leave the country; it was a thousand times worse than when Delphine had disappeared. He now works in a café-brasserie in a remote and rugged part of the Languedoc, where sometimes, after dinner, he can still make his neighbours rock with laughter as he tells them the one about the fat lady and the *terrine du petit chat*.

Ostracised in Barwell, struck off the Register, Felix Growcott moved back to London and lived for a while on the proceeds of his best-selling *Individual History of Gourmandism*. A couple of years later he fell ill, manifesting symptoms resembling those of senile dementia or Alzheimer's, although the autopsy later revealed it to have been Creutzfeldt-Jakob's disease. He was nursed by the last of his Circes to the bitter end, and left her all his money.

Valerie Farewell miscarried on the day of Roger Saddington's death. Soon after this, she and Thomas separated. She hung on to William so savagely that Judith shrugged her shoulders and went off to read Biology at Bristol. There she shared a room in her first year with Bryony Growcott, who had managed to gain a place in French and Philosophy.

Valerie stayed on in Barwell, becoming increasingly reclusive, and is currently engaged in a battle with the local authorities because she refuses to let five-year-old William attend Infant School.

At Valerie's insistence, Thomas Farewell sold up, left their house and went to live in a flat over a kebab shop on the other side of Stokeridge. He had lost his stomach for the business anyway. He has subsisted since then on the proceeds from the sale of the shop eked out by what he earns from casual labouring jobs. He drinks too much. He is plagued with atrocious nightmares about being lost in a forest where the trees whisper the name of his little girl, his ewe lamb, while their trunks sweat scarlet moisture.